WITCHLIGHT

*To Frankie,
my little, furry writing companion.*

First published in the UK in 2025 by Usborne Publishing Limited., Usborne House, 83-85 Saffron Hill, London EC1N 8RT, England, usborne.com

Usborne Verlag, Usborne Publishing Ltd., Prüfeninger Str. 20, 93049 Regensburg, Deutschland, VK Nr. 17560

Text copyright © Dominique Valente, 2025

The right of Dominique Valente to be identified as the author of this work has been asserted by her in accordance with the Copyright, Designs and Patents Act, 1988.

Illustrations by Eleonora Asparuhova © Usborne Publishing Limited, 2025

The name Usborne and the Balloon logo are Trade Marks of Usborne Publishing Limited.

All rights reserved. No part of this publication may be reproduced or used in any manner for the purpose of training artificial intelligence technologies or systems (including for text or data mining), stored in retrieval systems or transmitted in any form or by any means without prior permission of the publisher.

This is a work of fiction. The characters, incidents, and dialogues are products of the author's imagination and are not to be construed as real. Any resemblance to actual events or persons, living or dead, is entirely coincidental.

A CIP catalogue record for this book is available from the British Library.

ISBN 9781805316800 9443/1 JFMAMJJA OND/25

Printed and bound using 100% renewable electricity by CPI Group (UK) Ltd, CR0 4YY

WITCHLIGHT

DOMINIQUE VALENTE
ILLUSTRATED BY ELEONORA ASPARUHOVA

PAMPHLETS FOR THE PEOPLE

THE TRUTH
ABOUT THE
"ISLE-SPARK" MAGIC TEST

THE LIE WE'VE BEEN SOLD
BY THE DEPARTMENT WHO
BINDS OUR CHILDREN'S MAGIC

MISS HEGOTTY'S
SOCIETY PRESS

The Weekly Spellcast

THE FALL OF THE WHISTLEWITCH

For years, tales of the fierce defender of our seas, the infamous military sorcerer the "Whistlewitch", have inspired countless adventure stories. So why, then, did she risk her position as one of the Magic Isles' most prominent generals to kidnap Lord Persicaria Bury and attempt to steal a magical home? And what about her insistence that she didn't work alone? If that is true, why hasn't she named her accomplice? See page 3.

MAGICAL CREATURES DEMAND EQUAL RIGHTS TO HUMANS!

Troubles between magical creatures and the Department have escalated. Ever since the Great Quake released "isle-spark" (the magic that awoke dragons, wyverns and other mystical creatures from stone, forever transforming our nation), ensuring harmony between all hasn't been easy. "Most of us just want to get on with our lives and be treated the same as everyone else, that's all we ask," said Knox, a dragon, and owner of a coffee shop and bookstore in Edinburgh. Edel Scareweed, Royal Isle-Spark Military (RISM) spokesperson, said, "It is not as simple as 'equal rights for all', which probably seems lovely to people who aren't in the habit of using their brains – we need to remember that these are bloodthirsty, dangerous beasts, who want to take over our world!" See page 9.

A SECRET SOCIETY OF WITCHES?

Miss Hegotty has long caused Departmental headaches with her banned magical-correspondence course. But now it appears that she is behind a new secret society of witches who are distributing "truth pamphlets" that accuse the Department of binding children's magic! Something that has hit a nerve with parents, as fewer children than ever are "spark-touched" these days. It is believed that now only one in a hundred girls have magic, a big change from a decade ago, when it was around half of all girls. A Department spokesperson said, "We will not dignify Miss Hegotty's accusation with an answer. But we will remind everyone thinking of joining her highly ILLEGAL society that you risk being branded Ungovernable and if caught face SERIOUS CONSEQUENCES." See page 2.

THE GREAT SPARK-CLOCK – A MARVEL OF ISLE-SPARK INNOVATION!

After the fire that broke out earlier this year, burning down half of the Palace of Westminster (where, mercifully, the only loss sustained was to a warehouse full of Departmental records) the lightning-fast restoration of the buildings has been hailed as a "marvel of isle-spark technology". With the cherry on the cake being the installation of the Great Spark-Clock that some have begun calling "Big Ben", which is actually the name of its great bell. See page 15.

1
Trouble at the Headquarters of Miss Hegotty's Secret Society of Witches
1834, Huswyvern, Felixstowe

Autumn arrived ready to pick a fight. The wind took bites, the cold air slapped, and in a small fishing village, above the sea cliffs, an old gothic house shivered miserably in its boots.

Its name was Huswyvern, and right now it was trying *really* hard not to sneeze.

It wasn't going well.

This was particularly bad timing on Hus's part, as the weekly meeting for Miss Hegotty's Secret Society of Witches was about to start.

So far, apart from thirteen-year-old Eglantine, and Arthur the wyvern-butler, who both lived in Huswyvern, only Princess Victoria, and Eglantine's cousin, Eoin, had arrived. They were still waiting for the other society members to come through the portal door that magically connected the quiet seaside home in Suffolk to the bustling city of London.

Thanks to the magical bond Eglantine shared with her sentient house, she could usually sense what it was feeling, and what she sensed made her panic.

"Batten down the hatches! Hus is about to *blow*!"

"Oh, no!" cried Victoria. "Not again!"

This wasn't the first time they'd suffered the consequences of one of Huswyvern's sneezes. The cold it had been battling over the past few weeks had caused no end of trouble. Everyone braced themselves, planting their feet wide and holding on to chairs and paintings. Eglantine patted the wall in a soothing sort of way, her heart twisting with worry for her beloved home.

Arthur went to fetch a bucket of sand to put out the flames in the fireplace. Eoin, who had a rat on his shoulder (who may or may not have been the poet Lord Byron cursed into rodent form), kept one hand on a vase, and another on a spark-typewriter from which Hus was busy typing "Woe is me" in a rather pathetic fashion.

At least that was what Hus *tried* to type. But the letter M and O jammed. This seemed to be one of the other side effects of Hus's cold, so what the jammed keys typed instead was:

We is e

Which no one could understand, much to Hus's frustration.

When at last Huswyvern couldn't hold its sneeze any longer, the house made the equivalent of an *achoo* sound, which played out in the chords of creaking wood, hissing pipes, and the rattle and tinkle of glass.

Eoin yelped, "Look out!"

Part of the floor was now snaking up the walls, the windows had moved to the ground, and most terrifying of all – the fireplace was raining fire from its new, rather mad, position on the ceiling, as Hus had sneezed before Arthur could put the flames out.

Arthur flew up with the bucket of sand, while Eglantine and Victoria screamed and scuttled backwards, narrowly missing the flames.

Rat Lord Byron muttered (in the language of rats) that it was far too early in the day for this sort of nonsense, and dived back inside Eoin's pocket.

"All hands on deck," hollered the carved figure of the one-armed battle hero, Sorcerer Nelson, from his post above the mantelpiece.

Hus had never explained exactly why the enchanted figure of Sorcerer Nelson magically appeared on the wooden panelling one day when Eglantine was a little girl, but she guessed that the house had somehow summoned an echo of the naval hero as a kind of mentor of sorts for her.

In a world that so often tried to tell her she wasn't good enough because of the way she had been born (with one hand), Sorcerer Nelson, who had lost his arm and one of his eyes early on in his career, was a daily reminder that being different didn't

mean you couldn't achieve remarkable things. To this day, Sorcerer Nelson was considered the greatest naval officer in the nation's history. He'd prevented the powerful French Emperor, Napoleon, from invading the Magic Isles, and stealing its precious resource – isle-spark – which gave the isles their power.

Whenever Eglantine felt down because someone had said something pitying or mean about her arm, Arthur, who like Hus was her biggest supporter, would say, "They would do well to remember that if it wasn't for a one-handed person, the Magic Isles might have been conquered by the French."

But right now Eglantine wasn't thinking about any of that, as Sorcerer Nelson commanded them to, "Step lively and save the good ship *Victory!*" (he didn't quite understand that he wasn't aboard his battleship any more), she was too busy following his instructions. She wasn't the only one.

Arthur spread sand from the bucket onto the flames, and Victoria slowed the fire, using her magic which manipulated time. But she couldn't stop the heavy clouds of thick, black smoke that made them all cough and splutter, their eyes turning red.

Huswyvern opened up its windows, but as these were now on the floor, this didn't do much to clear the smoke.

Using her own powers, which combined her love of painting and flowers, Eglantine created several large, whirligig daisies by drawing them in the air with her fingers.

The giant flowers spun their petals and fanned some of the smoke from the room.

Eoin, who had just begun his magic lessons, and hadn't yet

discovered his Witchspark (a signature power that witches and wizards could unlock within themselves, given the right training), ran to the door and swung it open and closed, which was the best solution of all, proving that practicality really is a magic of its own.

But they had other problems to deal with, namely the topsy-turvy room they were left with.

Huswyvern was on it, though.

There was a scrape and a clang and a stomp as a coat rack, a chaise longue, an armoured suit, as well as a pair of old and worn magical shoes known simply as The Boots (who had long ago lost their heart to Arthur) rushed inside to clean up the mess.

The armoured suit rammed itself against the walls, which quickly straightened themselves out, while The Boots kicked at the floor until it slid back into place, and the windows, possibly feeling a bit ashamed of themselves, slunk back into position too.

When it was all over, the coat rack rushed forward to dust off Eglantine, who was covered in a fine layer of soot, while the chaise longue scuttled towards the future queen, eager to offer her a seat after her ordeal.

"What am I, chopped liver?" asked Eoin. The only assistance he was given was a kick by The Boots to get out the way so that the fireplace could hop back to its usual position.

Despite everything, Eglantine couldn't help chuckling when she saw Eoin's expression of outrage.

"You know Eoin is family, right?" she reminded her magical house. "You will have to eventually forgive him, you know?"

There was a *harrumph-creak* from the door, and this time it wasn't just Eglantine who laughed.

Eoin had made the mistake of not showing the right level of enthusiasm for the room Hus had decorated especially for him a few weeks ago, and Hus had been frosty towards him ever since.

(In Eoin's defence, Hus *had* papered the walls with giant, terrifying sketches of rats, having somewhat overestimated the boy's affection for Rat Lord Byron...)

As far as Eglantine was concerned, one of the best things that had come out of last year was finding her long-lost cousin, Eoin, and making an unlikely new friend in the princess.

Eoin worked in Kensington Palace, and had been the one to witness the moment Victoria discovered she had a magical power and had frozen everyone in the palace in time, apart from him. Royals in the Magic Isles were forbidden to have magic, but instead of turning her in, he had decided to help Victoria, and applied to Miss Hegotty's banned magical course for aspiring witches on her behalf so that she might learn to control her ability and keep it a secret. Victoria and Eoin became firm friends. Victoria helped him discover who his father was (Eglantine's uncle, Lichen) which had (along with Miss Hegotty's guiding hand) led them to Eglantine and Huswyvern.

Back then, Eglantine had her own problems. She didn't have magic, which was a major issue, considering that she needed a Witchspark to create the bond with her magical home and keep it out of the hands of her uncle.

It turned out that Uncle Lichen had secretly arranged for

Eglantine's magic to be bound when she was very young. Eglantine had grown up believing she didn't have any powers at all, something her uncle planned to use to his benefit so that it would be easier to steal Huswyvern from her after her mother died.

Last year, he'd almost succeeded. He'd partnered with a powerful sorcerer named the Whistlewitch, who kidnapped Eglantine's father and tried to ransom him in exchange for the house.

Luckily, thanks to Miss Hegotty's lessons, Eglantine was able to finally unlock her magic and make the unbreakable bond with her house. Together with her new friends, she defeated her uncle and the Whistlewitch, and got her father back.

That was when Miss Hegotty had told them about her secret society, which fights against magical crimes and injustice, and Huswyvern had volunteered to become its headquarters. But today, the thing that was most concerning the members was Huswyvern itself, and its worsening cold.

Arthur took a handkerchief out of his waistcoat pocket and began to wipe his face and his pince-nez free of soot. "You really know how to bring excitement to the weekly meeting, Hus," he joked. "At least this time we've still got the roof."

At their last meeting, the entire roof had blown *off*. While that had been scary, it wasn't nearly as bad as today.

Eglantine winced. "I think Huswyvern is getting worse."

Arthur nodded. There was worry in his eyes too.

Everyone looked at each other, feeling a bit helpless. Everything they had tried so far had failed.

"I really thought the last healing spell would work," said Victoria sadly.

Eglantine sighed. "Me too."

It was the third one they'd tried over the past month. The coat rack rubbed Eglantine's back as if to say it was alright.

Suddenly, the spark-typewriter atop the table clacked out a word. But the letter E jammed as it did. Hus gave a little frustrated sigh.

Spll

They all turned to look at the spark-typewriter in surprise.

"Spll? Do you mean 'spell'?" asked Eglantine.

The coat rack nodded.

Arthur brightened. "That's the spirit, Hus. There must be another spell we can try."

"Remember, it is always darkest before dawn," agreed Sorcerer Nelson.

"I'll check the Grimoire again later," said Eglantine, feeling her spirits rise too. They were right. There was no reason to despair just yet.

Suddenly Eoin's face looked puzzled as he stared at something behind them. "Do you think that's a problem?" he asked, pointing to the portal door. "Considering we're still expecting the other society members to arrive?"

Eglantine turned to see what Eoin was pointing at and frowned. The London portal door had *moved*.

In the pandemonium, she had forgotten about the other society members.

What if they'd tried to use the portal door when Hus sneezed?

"It's just a bit out of place, though, I mean, how bad could it be?" asked Victoria.

Bad, as it turned out.

2

UNDERCOVER MISSION

They discovered *just* how bad soon afterwards.

"The p-o-o-rtal was miles away from where it usually is beneath Big Ben," wheezed Miss Luthuli as she and her daughter, Nandi, made their way inside half an hour later.

Miss Luthuli was an accomplished botanist and Eglantine's late mother's best friend. She and her daughter, ten-year-old Nandi, had helped Eglantine and the others thwart Eglantine's uncle, Lichen, and the sorcerer he'd partnered with to steal Huswyvern the year before. Afterwards, when they heard about Miss Hegotty's secret society and its mission, they were quick to join.

Placing the portal to Miss Hegotty's Secret Society of Witches right under the noses of the Department of Isle-Spark Regulation was a cheeky move on Huswyvern's part, but it had done that specifically so that the society could keep an eye on the Department.

Eoin stared at the new arrivals in surprise. "The portal moved to a new place entirely? Where was it?" he asked, shocked.

"To-o-wer Bridge!" puffed Miss Luthuli, still a bit out of breath, as she pulled out a chair on the long wooden meeting table and sat down rather wearily.

Eglantine gulped. "But that's miles away! How could the portal have moved that much, when the door here is only slightly off-centre?" She looked at the door in confusion.

Sorcerer Nelson was the one who answered: "Magic and navigation have similar mechanics. If you are only off-course by a few degrees you can land in an entirely different place. Did I ever tell you about the time we ended up in Madagascar by mistake? It was a bright spring morning, dawn had just crept over the horizon and I saw a bird of a most unusual plumage—"

"Perhaps another time, Sorcerer." Eglantine cut him off before he could get started on one of his many battle yarns (which could go on for a while).

"How did you even *find* the portal?" asked Victoria. "It must have been like searching for a needle in a haystack."

"Quite! But Nandi had a stroke of genius, with a plan that made the door sing for us. She just followed the sound of the music till we found its source."

"What? How?" cried Victoria.

They all turned to look at the younger girl, who blushed.

"It was sort of thanks to you, Eglantine," she said.

"Me?" said Eglantine, shocked.

Nandi bit her lip. "I saw one of your intermediate lessons on the table the other day, and tried it out on the portal door."

Eoin gasped. "You just decided you would try a locator charm you glanced at last week – and it *worked*?"

Nandi nodded, a bit sheepishly.

Eoin scoffed. "Well, that's just delightful. For *you*."

Everyone snorted. Nandi's ease with magic was unusual, and unfortunately it hadn't come as easily to them. Victoria was in the unique position of having to go about things back to front. Her Witchspark power had erupted without her understanding basic elementary magic first, so she was having to learn the foundations now in order to be able to harness other forms of magic.

Eglantine was a bit further along than the others; she was halfway through Miss Hegotty's intermediate course. Her eyes widened. "You tried the Lost Charm Spell on the door?" she guessed.

"Yes. I was shocked when it actually worked – I remembered that only the person who cast the charm would be able hear its song, so I thought it would be worth trying if we wanted to look for it..."

"Brilliant," said Eglantine and Victoria together, while Eoin whistled, impressed.

"That was clever thinking," came a voice from behind. "And if there's one thing I value, it's thinking fast when in a tight spot."

They all turned in surprise.

It was Miss Hegotty.

No one had heard her enter.

Nandi wasn't the only one who found herself standing up straight.

Even Huswyvern smartened itself up: shaking itself free of dust, applying a bit of spit and polish to the windows (there was a squeaking sort of sound that accompanied this and the glass soon sparkled) and righting the paintings on the walls.

Sorcerer Nelson saluted her like he would a fellow sorcerer.

Miss Hegotty had that sort of effect.

Not that she seemed that aware of it, or if she was, she didn't comment. She merely accepted the chair that pulled itself out in front of her at the head of the table, and smiled warmly at them all.

Eglantine had known Miss Hegotty for a year now, but she still couldn't stop the thrill of nervous excitement that shot through her whenever Miss Hegotty was here, in her house. She was, after all, the witch who topped the Department's list of most wanted witches.

"I believe, if we're all ready, we can call the meeting to order," said Miss Hegotty.

The spark-typewriter's keys clicked to show that it was primed to take the notes of their meeting. Several typewriter keys got stuck together, but Hus soldiered on.

"Our truth pamphlets have been working. More people than ever are questioning why only boys from wealthy families seem to get magic now. Some families are starting to test their children for magic at home. So, of course, it will come as no surprise that home magic-testing devices are now banned as well," said Miss Hegotty.

This was the reason the society had been formed: to expose what the Department of Isle-Spark Regulation were doing – which was deliberately, secretly and illegally binding the magic of people like Eglantine and Eoin (girls, or boys who came from poor backgrounds) so that only boys from wealthy families got magic. They wanted to ensure that power stayed in the hands of wealthy men.

For the past year, their society had been hard at work, trying to gather the evidence they needed to expose the Department's wrongdoings and ensure magic was free and fair for all.

"That's good news," said Eglantine.

"Why is that good?" asked Nandi, looking at Eglantine in confusion. "Surely it's bad if the Department are banning home magic tests?"

Eglantine shook her head. "Not necessarily. The fact that it's made the Banned List shows that it's a real concern for the Department. It proves that more people than usual must be testing their children's magic at home. People are beginning to see that what we're saying about the Department is true. The Department really are binding children's magic, and this isn't some crackpot conspiracy theory by some bonkers society who want to overthrow the government."

"Speak for yourself," joked Arthur.

They all laughed. Especially considering Arthur was the one least likely to ever break a rule out of all of them. He may look like a fierce, small dragon, but Arthur was a stickler for the rules, happiest at home with his talons curled up around a good book. He would rather read about battles than actually wage them... but they were facing a battle now, to be sure. All of them.

Being part of an illegal society or signing up to Miss Hegotty's course wasn't something any of them had done lightly. But someone had to expose the Department and its warped way of keeping power and magic only in the hands of the wealthy elite.

Miss Hegotty nodded. "Eglantine is right. The fact that so many people are willing to risk the Department's ire to acquire these home magic tests is good news indeed. They are starting to see that the Department is corrupt.

"Even from within the Department, there are those who are aware that things are not being run as they should. I have made contact with a frustrated minister, Mrs Kusum, who, like us, has been trying to figure out who is behind these awful practices so that they can be brought to task. Unfortunately, until she has proof, there is not much she and her supporters can do. They are a small group with not much power yet, and they have taken an enormous risk in speaking with me.

"So, if we want to protect children it's up to us; we are going to have to find out *how* the Department is binding their magic. And for that, I have a plan."

There was excited murmuring all around.

"I have long had a sense that magic testing centres are linked to the binding process in some way, but my theory has proved difficult to investigate as these centres are so difficult to enter unless you are an official Department worker. Which is why this seems like an opportunity far too good to miss!"

She waved her fingers, and a folded-up newspaper appeared out of nowhere to land on top of the table, straight onto a page that read: *Job Vacancies*.

"I am proposing an undercover mission," she said.

Miss Hegotty waved her hand and two job advertisements were circled in red.

WANTED: ADMINISTRATOR AT ISLE-SPARK MAGICAL TESTING CENTRE, WESTMINSTER
Responsible for checking off names of children attending the tests, as well as other light administration duties. Training will be provided. Send letters of application to Moss Hollingsworth, Department of Isle-Spark Regulation.

WANTED: TEA PERSON AT ISLE-SPARK MAGICAL TESTING CENTRE, WESTMINSTER
Responsible for making tea and sandwiches. Send letters of application to Moss Hollingsworth, Department of Isle-Spark Regulation.

Eglantine frowned. "Are you saying some of us should apply for these jobs?"

Miss Hegotty tapped the advertisements with a fingernail. "Yes, myself and Ayanda, if she's amenable?" She looked at Miss Luthuli and grinned. "You could put your famous acting skills to use."

Last year, thanks to a spell Eglantine cast, Miss Luthuli took on the appearance of Eglantine's father when the royals came for a visit and no one was any the wiser. Well, until the spell wore off and all hell broke loose...

"I'm always game for a bit of theatrics," said Miss Luthuli. "I'm guessing we will need a false identity each, as well as some kind of a disguise, something that lasts longer than the glamour spell, though."

Miss Hegotty gave a wry smile. "I have some ideas."

"But how will you guarantee that you get the jobs?" asked Arthur.

Miss Hegotty raised a brow and the wyvern turned a darker shade of green in embarrassment. Sometimes, just for a moment, they forgot Miss Hegotty was *that* Miss Hegotty – the most feared and powerful outlaw-witch in the Magic Isles.

But the witch only looked amused. "Oh, don't worry about that, Arthur – I have ways and means to ensure that our applications are the only ones that are considered."

Eglantine thought of how Miss Hegotty placed "wild adverts" in newspapers that promoted her lessons and the way she had hoodwinked the post office to deliver her course – things the

Department had tried for years to put a stop to but couldn't. This, by comparison, seemed easy.

They all nodded.

"We will need another volunteer so that we see all angles of the testing centre – a child who must experience the magic test itself, so we can trial my theory that they are bound while at the centre."

"I can do that," said Eglantine. "I can use a spell to make myself appear younger—"

To her disappointment, Miss Hegotty shook her head. "I was thinking that Nandi would make more sense in this case. Her Witchspark – the ability to shapeshift – will allow her to turn into a different child each day, therefore we could get a real sense of how these testing centres operate."

Eglantine nodded but had to squash a twinge of envy at the idea of missing out on such an exciting mission. She knew it made sense for them to use Nandi instead, who had only recently discovered her shapeshifting Witchspark and it was already proving very useful.

"Will you need the rest of us to act as lookouts?" asked Eoin.

Miss Hegotty shook her head, and Eglantine's feeling of being left out intensified.

"I think it's best that you and Victoria continue with what you have been doing – find out what Sir Conroy and his secret meetings with Lord Ragwort are about."

Sir Conroy was the comptroller at Kensington Palace in charge of running the household and finances, and he was one of the reasons Victoria's life was so restricted. He ruled with an iron fist, ensuring that she had very little freedom. Conroy was also a great friend of Lord Ragwort's, who was the former leader of the Royal Isle-Spark Military and current head of the Banned Magic Office. Ragwort had been visiting the palace regularly to see Conroy. Victoria was sure they were plotting something. Once, Victoria had been convinced that they had been discussing her, by the way they stared when they passed her in the corridor.

"I think Lord Ragwort is using some sort of spell that blocks magic as I couldn't use my powers on them to get inside the study or hear them at all."

Miss Hegotty nodded. "That makes sense."

"But we did hear him say something about 'it all coming into alignment'," said Eoin. "Which definitely sounds like they are up to something."

Victoria nodded. "Then Conroy saw me, and they started speaking about a flu outbreak – everyone in the palace always panics whenever it's flu season as they're afraid that if I catch a cold, I'll spontaneously combust or something…"

The others grinned. Victoria had told them how Conroy and her mother were hypochondriacs when it came to her health. Each had different reasons, though.

Victoria's mother cared about her, while Conroy wanted to make sure that Victoria lived long enough to become queen one day, because if she didn't he would be out of a job.

"Do you think Sir Conroy knows someone in the Department is binding children's magic?" Nandi asked.

"I don't know," said Miss Hegotty. "But finding out whatever it is they're meeting about could be useful to us. So, stay safe, but I think it's important you and Eoin keep trying to find out what they are really up to."

Victoria and Eoin nodded.

Miss Hegotty turned to address Eglantine. "I'm sure your focus will be on helping Huswyvern, Eglantine," she said.

Eglantine felt a prickle of shame. Did Miss Hegotty think she was planning to abandon Hus? She would *never* do that. It was her top priority to cure Hus of this cold. She had just thought that somehow she could do that *and* be a part of this new undercover mission at the testing centre... It felt like everyone else had important assignments for the society apart from her and Arthur.

If Miss Hegotty thought Hus's condition needed her sole focus, she must think it's serious. The thought made her stomach churn slightly. She touched the chair, seeking reassurance, and it reached out to squeeze her hand in return.

"I'll keep checking the Grimoire, and I am also waiting for the caretakers of the other two sentient homes to get back to me. I wrote to ask if they'd encountered any similar illnesses in the past and if they might have information or a remedy they would be willing to share."

"That was good thinking," said Miss Luthuli.

"Thanks," said Eglantine.

"I will have another task for you and Arthur in the next few weeks, though," said Miss Hegotty.

They turned to her in surprise.

"I will need you to welcome a new member of the society."

"A new member! Who?" cried Victoria.

Miss Hegotty stared into the middle distance for a moment. Then: "I can't say who just yet. But I have a sense that she is the part of the puzzle we need to go forward. She holds some key part we haven't yet realized is important... Unfortunately, I don't know what that is at the moment. Which is frustrating. But I sense that things will become clearer in time."

Instead of being confused, Eglantine and Victoria shared a knowing sort of look.

It wasn't the first time Miss Hegotty had given them vague instructions that all seemed to link up somehow to a greater part of a plan.

"Is that your Witchspark?" asked Eoin. "You can see the future?"

They had all wondered about this in the past, but none of them had been bold enough to ask. Eglantine's eyes widened at Eoin's daring.

Miss Hegotty shook her head. "No, I can sense when things fit together. But unfortunately, the pieces are just like a jigsaw, random, scattered and it takes ages to work out the overall picture. But some pieces are clearer than others, and our new member belongs in the centre of things. I can feel it."

They all stared at her in a kind of awe.

Miss Hegotty shrugged. "I wish it *was* the ability to see the future. It would be far simpler."

They laughed.

"What I can see, without any need for a crystal ball, is that the Department has made it their mission to catch us, and now that we are taking more risks, we need to tighten our security measures.

"Eglantine and Hus have added to the wards along the perimeter of Huswyvern, so no one can enter, but there is still a chance we could be followed or overheard outside these walls, and so other protective means are necessary. Which is why we have developed these."

The spark-typewriter's metal bar resembled, for a moment, a cocked ear.

Then Miss Hegotty twirled her hand near her coat lapel, where a smattering of stars appeared and transformed into something else.

"Ayanda helped design them," she said, nodding her head towards Miss Luthuli, who smiled.

As Miss Hegotty spoke, a small flower blossomed on her coat. She twirled her fingers again and suddenly everyone had a different flower pinned to their clothes. It was the sort of decoration some people wore when they dressed up.

Arthur gasped. "I say, well, now, that looks *smart.*"

He was looking down at his waistcoat, where a spiky yet elegant bright-red flower was pinned.

Miss Luthuli cocked a brow. "It is smart in other ways too. Each of your flowers is coded to match you. Yours, dear Arthur, is antirrhinum."

Arthur let out a chuckle of recognition. "Ah – of course," said the wyvern. "Antirrhinum, also known as dragon flower – or snapdragon," he said, his eyes warm.

Eglantine stared at hers in wonder. It was a pale pink wild rose, and like Arthur she was able to guess the reason for hers – it was the flower that was her namesake – an eglantine rose.

Miss Luthuli's was a daisy, which she said was her favourite flower, and she told the others that Nandi's was a lily of the valley – a May flower because she was born in May. Victoria's was a purple violet, and Eoin's was a green patch of clover, for his Irish ancestry.

"The flowers aren't merely decorative," continued Miss Luthuli. "They can sense when one of us is in danger and let the rest of us know.

"If a threat is detected, all our protection flowers will change to resemble the flower of the person who is in danger. The flowers have a locator charm so that we should be able to find you if you are ever captured. It will then transform into a picture of the location so we can come to you."

Miss Hegotty touched her flower, which transformed from a small clump of purple blooms, her namesake, hepatica, into the multicoloured shape of an old gothic house. All the flowers fitted together like puzzle pieces to form a perfect miniature likeness of Huswyvern.

There were gasps of amazement as all their flowers transformed into the shape of Hus.

"If your flower looks like this, it means a meeting has been called. In light of Huswyvern's illness," said Miss Hegotty, "I think it would be best, from now on, if you wait for your flower to change into Hus before our regularly scheduled meetings so that we know it is safe to use the portal."

They all nodded.

"If Hus turns black, however," said Miss Hegotty, continuing, "it means it's not safe or Huswyvern is in danger," she explained, twisting her fingers over her flower to demonstrate.

Eglantine wasn't the only one who felt uneasy when she saw her flower turn black for a moment, before Miss Hegotty touched it again and it went back to normal.

She prayed they would never have to use *that* signal.

Before they left, Miss Hegotty, Nandi and Miss Luthuli went over their plans to infiltrate the Westminster Isle-Spark Magical Testing Centre. The stakes couldn't be higher for this particular mission, as they would be working undercover within a Department-run building, and the chances of them being caught were high. But it was worth it. If they could figure out how the Department were binding children's magic, they could finally prove what the Department were doing and thus help Mrs Kusum and her supporters.

But still, Eglantine couldn't help feeling left out. She knew looking after Hus deserved to be her priority, but it certainly wasn't as exciting as what the others had planned.

Victoria and Eoin were the last to leave.

"Do you have to go?" asked Eglantine.

"I'm afraid so," said Victoria with regret. "I had to freeze the palace in time, so Eoin and I could get away without anyone noticing. It's been over two hours now, and I'm not sure how much longer my magic will hold."

"You're telling me that the entire time you've been here they've all been frozen in time?" gasped Arthur, horrified.

Victoria raised a pair of crossed fingers. "Well, *hopefully*."

Eglantine snorted.

Victoria put her face in her hands. "I know, it's *awful*. If there was another way I could get away without anyone noticing, I'd try that. But short of creating a decoy Victoria it's the only way."

"It's not your fault," said Eoin hotly. "It's not like you want to suspend them all in time, it's the stupid 'Kensington System' that your mother and Sir Conroy created that means you can't be alone for more than five minutes."

He wasn't exaggerating.

Victoria's grandfather was king, and when her father died, she became next in line to the throne. As the queen-to-be, Victoria's life was heavily controlled. She was never alone; she couldn't even walk down the stairs without holding someone's hand in case she slipped.

Eglantine patted her shoulder in sympathy. She would never have imagined she could feel sorry for a royal, with so much wealth and privilege at her feet, but once you knew the truth about Victoria's life, and how oppressive it was, it was hard not to sympathize.

But magic had changed all that. Victoria's Witchspark gave

her freedom. But it clearly had its limitations. Freezing everyone in the palace for hours on end was incredibly risky.

"I know I should probably not risk coming here at all, but what we're doing is important," said Victoria. "I'm sure that whatever Conroy and Ragwort are up to can't be good."

The others nodded.

"I just wish I knew what."

"We will get to the bottom of it, Princess," assured Eoin.

She nodded.

Eglantine sighed. "If only there was an easier way to get you in and out of Huswyvern."

The mantelpiece seemed to frown in thought.

Victoria shrugged. "I know," she said, then turned to go through the portal door.

As she did, a large iron pin about the length of a child's palm detached itself from the portal keyhole, and landed, somehow, in Victoria's hair without anyone noticing, and she left taking a small part of Huswyvern with her.

A puzzle piece that seemed to have a mind of its own.

Not to mention, a plan.

3
FEVERS AND BEST-LAID PLANS

Later that night, Eglantine and Arthur were upstairs in the library, in their pyjamas, scanning the Huswyvern Grimoire for more healing spells for Huswyvern's cold.

Outside, the wind howled and the sea crashed against the rocks. But where they sat, in faded pink velvet armchairs facing a roaring, crackling fire, it was cosy. Particularly as Arthur had brought them two steaming cups of hot chocolate and a plate full of spiced biscuits.

The Boots were curled up lovingly at Arthur's feet, like a dog. On the bookshelves, several of the books were randomly opening themselves and hoping to capture their interest. One did a little shimmy, while another slammed itself shut and sulked after being persistently ignored.

Eglantine and Arthur didn't pay the library's antics much attention – they were too used to it – just like Eglantine didn't pay much attention to the way the house's ancient spellbook kept trying to flip to the back to show her a page that had been mostly ripped out, apart from a tiny triangular fragment. She was used to the Grimoire suggesting weird and wonderful spells to her, and she couldn't help thinking that perhaps it hadn't realized that the one it kept trying to suggest wasn't there any more.

A distant part of her mind noted that she was feeling a bit tired. She had a slight headache and her throat was sore, and the spot behind her neck, where a patch of skin was dry and itching, was bothering her. She knew what she needed was probably to rest, but she didn't have time to worry about herself – not while Hus was feeling so poorly. She'd rest when Hus was better.

She took a firm grip on the Grimoire and flicked back to the beginning, trying to focus on the task at hand. "The last spell I tried was to break a fever – but maybe Hus has more of a cold?" she asked Arthur, who nodded.

"It's possible."

There was a creak-like sigh from Hus, and the spellbook tried again, rather insistently, to flip towards the end of the book to the torn-out page. Eglantine frowned. Perhaps, on reflection, it was suggesting that they do nothing.

Eglantine kept a firm hand on the book. "Hus, earlier it seemed like you were trying to tell us there must be a spell we could try," she said, referring to when the spark-typewriter had typed and jammed itself on the word *spll*.

Eglantine wondered if, now that Hus was faced with the reality of trying a new spell (which wasn't always pleasant to experience), it had lost its enthusiasm. She rubbed the arm of her chair soothingly.

"I know the last remedy wasn't comfortable, but you almost seemed better for a little while afterwards," said Arthur in agreement. "We have to keep at it, Hus."

There was a *harrumph* from the floorboard. The last spell had involved dressing the house in several magically knitted jumpers, in the hopes that making it warm would break its fever. Huswyvern had turned an odd pinkish shade. The walls began to pool in sweat and after a while, Hus had catapulted the metres and metres of yarn that covered it from top to toe into the sea and made an odd whooshing sound as every part of it sighed in blessed, cool relief.

Eglantine turned a page, deep in thought. "I remember seeing something interesting – oh, here it is," she said, pausing at a familiar page and eagerly scanning the spell. "It's supposed to be the magical equivalent of a large dose of cod liver oil," she said, musing aloud.

There was a horrified shudder from the house and goosebumps emerged on the walls. The spellbook flipped quickly past the spell and reopened once more, this time with some degree of urgency, on the mostly torn-out page. She looked at it again, but really there was nothing there, just a few disjoined words she could barely read. Something about "the stars" and a "counter".

"I don't know why you keep showing me this page!"

But, of course, there was no answer from the book. Perhaps Hus hoped the cold would go away on its own – but they couldn't take that chance. The sneezes caused such chaos, and they were never sure what might go wrong next. Eglantine could sense that it was making Hus miserable, and she wanted so much to help it feel better...but at the moment, it just seemed to be getting worse.

She flicked back to the cod-liver-equivalent spell and kept a tight hold. After a while there was a sigh of resignation from the house.

Arthur peered over her shoulder. "It takes a week to brew, so you're safe for now, Hus," he told the house fondly.

There was another creaking *harrumph*, this time from the door.

Arthur sneezed. Then blew his nose with a handkerchief.

"Bless you. Hope you're not coming down with something too."

"Just the dust," said Arthur, waving a talon in dismissal. "I never get sick."

Eglantine grinned, as the cushion blew a raspberry at the wyvern. "Too right, Hus. Must be nice for some," she said, then winked at Arthur as she stood up. "I'd better get started, then."

Arthur was shocked. "It's nearly midnight! It would be better to start first thing tomorrow, after a good night's sleep."

Eglantine shook her head. "It says I need to pick river weeds after midnight when the dew is just beginning to form." She looked at the clock on the mantelpiece. "If I go now, I can get at least one of the ingredients, and then I promise I'll go straight to bed. I must admit I'm feeling a bit tuckered out."

Arthur sighed. "I'm not surprised. You've been burning the candle at both ends trying to help Hus. Your father made me promise that I would ensure that you got enough rest and weren't—"

Eglantine's lips quirked into a smile, as she guessed: "—being me?"

Arthur snorted. "Yes, well, only when it comes to staying up too late."

She nodded. She was a night owl at the best of times, but with Hus being ill, it meant she hadn't been getting much sleep lately.

Arthur grinned. "I said I'd *try*," he admitted. "I never promised him I would succeed."

Eglantine grinned back. "I'm sure he knows that."

Eglantine was a very determined sort of person, something she thought was one of the advantages of having been born with one hand. Growing up, she'd been told that some things might be impossible for her – like tying her shoelaces, doing her hair, putting on a watch, skipping a rope or riding a spark-bicycle. She had found that so long as she was willing to keep trying, and looking for different solutions to problems – like using a bangle to hold the skipping rope in her little arm – it was funny how little turned out to actually be *impossible*. She did all of those things and more, just in her own way.

Being stubborn to a fault helped there too. When she got it into her mind to do something, like learn a new spell, or help

Huswyvern get over its cold, she found it difficult to know when to stop, and that included when to go to sleep.

Arthur might have been her best friend, but he was also, for the time being, her guardian, and he took that role, as he did most things, seriously.

Her father was a curator for the History of Isle-Spark Museum in London and his new job involved a significant amount of travel across the Isles, tracking down rare and priceless isle-spark artefacts and books. He was currently in Wales, where someone had donated their library and he was sorting through all the books.

Eglantine said, "I'll be as quick as I can through the London portal to get the river weeds."

Arthur stifled a yawn, then got up too. "I'll come with you. I don't like the idea of you being alone and out so late."

Eglantine waved a hand. "What I need is just outside the portal door, Arthur. Go on up to bed. I'll only be a minute or two, I promise."

"What if Hus sneezes again?" he asked worriedly.

"I doubt it would. Huswyvern doesn't generally seem to sneeze twice in a day."

Arthur shot her a look. "Let's hope it stays that way."

"Don't worry, off to bed with you. I won't be long."

Arthur nodded.

But, as it turned out, Arthur had every reason to worry.

4

A Sneeze in Time

It was quiet along the River Thames. The stars were blanketed by fog and cloud, but a pinprick moon provided enough light for Eglantine as she walked along the river. The vast and beautiful parliament buildings, which had recently been restored after a great fire a few months before, were reflected back in the water.

The giant bell, Big Ben, chimed the midnight hour as Eglantine snipped off a set of dew-soaked weeds and put them in a basket.

She turned back towards the portal at the foot of the clock building, when the last chime rang out. The cobbled street was deserted, apart from a distant carriage that was going past in the opposite direction.

No one saw the young girl with long blond hair, wrapped in her mother's old cloak as she hastened towards the door only she seemed able to see.

As soon as her fingers touched the handle though, she felt it. Hus was about to sneeze. Her heart clenched in fear and before she could do anything, it was too late. Her world began to spin.

Eglantine cried out, "Wait! Hus, please stop!"

But there was no stopping this.

When, at last, the portal quit spinning, she landed on her back, rather hard, the wind knocked out of her.

After a moment, she sat up dizzily, feeling sick and terrified. She had no idea where she was. The thought of being lost somewhere far from home caused her throat to turn dry.

But then she recognized the panelling in the parlour room. She was still in Huswyvern.

"Oh, Hus," she breathed, touching the floor. "You gave me such a fright."

She sprung her hand back in shock. Hus didn't feel like Hus *at all*. It felt…almost like a stranger.

The connection, their bond, was gone.

Her heart beat wildly inside her chest.

This Huswyvern wasn't the Huswyvern she knew.

It wasn't like the glitches from before. It was something else entirely.

There were other changes too, changes she hadn't noticed at first because she'd been too dizzy. As her vision cleared, she looked around in confusion.

An old grandfather clock, its face painted with stars and moons, let out a single chime.

She remembered that clock from when she was a little girl. The last time she'd seen it like that, whole and upright, at around age four, she had been playing a game with the footstool and she had gone hurtling into the clock so hard that it toppled over. It would have landed right on her if Hus hadn't acted as quickly as it did. The footstool shoved her out of harm's way, taking most of the impact as the clock crashed to the floor. Even so a tiny piece of glass had hit her on the forehead, leaving behind a small scar.

Eglantine felt the raised edge of it now, and looked at the clock in wonder.

Hus had been the one to banish the clock from the room. It never bothered to repair it, as if it had wanted to punish it for daring to hurt her. Eglantine had always felt a little guilty about that. It hadn't been the clock's fault that she'd fallen into it.

She had asked Hus a few times if it would bring the clock back, but it refused. She knew it was because it felt bad about what happened.

Why would Hus have brought it back now, though?

She frowned as she looked around.

It wasn't the only thing that had changed.

It was the same room, the same parlour they used as their society headquarters. But it was different, and not in the mad way it had been earlier, with things out of place. The table and chairs were gone. Instead there was a sofa, a small card table and several dusty armchairs. The carving of Sorcerer Nelson wasn't in the panelling near the fireplace and she missed his assured presence. If nothing else, he'd have a theory about what was going on. The walls next to the panelling were covered in a faded-looking floral wallpaper, a pattern she vaguely remembered from when she was small.

Her brain struggled to understand what she was seeing and feeling, besides the fact that it was all *wrong*.

A large spider with a red dot on its body scuttled along the floor and, from somewhere she couldn't see, she heard a soft rustling sound. She glanced around, trying to find the source.

To her shock she saw a blond, skinny boy wearing an old-fashioned ruffled shirt, with an ink stain on the left sleeve, sitting hunched in the padded window seat around the corner, partially hidden behind one of the heavy red curtains. The window offered a bright and sunny view of the cliffs and the rolling sea crashing below.

Who is he? What is he doing here? she thought, while another part of her brain wondered how it could have become daylight so quickly.

She was about to ask the boy hotly what he was doing in her house, but the way he appeared so furtive, kept glancing over his shoulder, as if he was afraid of being caught, intrigued her. She wanted to see what he was reading first.

She stepped forward, only for her shoe to squeak on the wooden floor. The boy startled. He yelped when he saw her.

"Who are you? Where did you come from?" he demanded.

He made to shove the book away, out of sight, and Eglantine

clean forgot that she had been trying to see what he was reading. She was too busy staring at his face in horror.

No, she thought, her stomach churning.

It can't be.

But she would recognize those cold eyes anywhere.

He was at least twenty years younger than the last time she had seen him.

Uncle Lichen.

He was closer to her age now.

Her heart pounded. After last year, and the things he'd put her through, she had hoped she would never have to see him again.

She stared at him in disbelief, temporarily losing the power of speech.

He seemed to suffer from no such problems. "I asked you a question! I demand to know what you are doing here!" he screeched. His pale face twisted in outrage. "Who said you could enter this house?" Then his nose wrinkled in apparent disgust. "Ugh, what happened to your arm?"

She flinched. She had known for years how her uncle felt about her. Part of the reason he'd tried so hard to steal Huswyvern away from her was that he didn't think she deserved it because of the way she'd been born. That someone in her family thought that way about her had always been a source of pain. She doubted that feeling would ever go away, but somewhere beyond it came a bubbling up of anger, like a dam about to burst. How dare he come into her *home* and look at her that way? She shouldn't have to take him saying things like that anywhere, but she certainly didn't need to take it *here* in *her* house!

She realized, despite her fury, that he didn't know who she was, but she didn't owe him her story. He didn't have a right to know what had happened to her arm just because she was different. No one did.

"First of all, what am *I* doing here?" snapped Eglantine. "More like, what are *you* doing here? How did you trick Huswyvern into letting you in? Did you use some youth potion to make yourself younger?"

He should never have been able to even cross the threshold without her permission and yet here he was. She couldn't believe that Hus would ever fall for one of his tricks again.

"What are you talking about? I live here! Why would I need a youth potion? I'm twelve! And I wouldn't need magic, even if I had it, to get inside my own house! Are you unwell, or are you some kind of a ghost? You look like a ghost to me. Helli is too soft, I've told her she needs to banish the lot of you. The Vikings are the worst, are you one of them? Is that what happened to your arm? Did you lose it in a battle?"

Eglantine's nostrils flared in irritation. For a moment, she was tempted to tell him that she was a special kind of Valkyrie who took nasty boys like him to the other, not-so heavenly, place, but she resisted the impulse.

His words, however, made her frown.

Why does he think I'm a ghost?

She looked down at herself, only to gasp. She was almost

transparent! Like she was a living but faded version of herself. She could even see through her hand a little. She gulped. What was going on?

It was like a nightmare. Only this was real.

There was the sound of footsteps and then...she saw her mother. She was a little older than Eglantine was now.

Eglantine was used to seeing her mother at various ages, because in the years since her mother had died she had come to visit her in ghost form at different stages of her life. But this was no ghost. This was the flesh and blood, real-life version of her mother's younger self.

They were almost the same height and her hair had a kink in it just like Eglantine's did.

That was when at last she understood what had happened, what had gone wrong with the portal this time when Huswyvern sneezed.

It took me back in time.

Her heart thrashed inside in her chest as she realized the enormity of what had happened. While a small part of her was thrilled to see her mother in the flesh, the idea of being stuck in the past as a kind of ghost was, frankly, *terrifying*.

"Can we help you?" asked Heliotrope, far more polite than Lichen. Only to gasp in sudden horror as she looked from Lichen to Eglantine accusingly, when she noticed what her brother was holding behind his back. "Did you help him to open it – is he trying to sell it to you?!"

"Open what?" cried Eglantine. "I'm not here to buy anything!"

Before Helli could respond, Eglantine's world began to spin once more, and the next thing she knew she was outside the London portal door, being violently ill at the foot of Big Ben. When the world stopped spinning at last, she could smell the briny, river scent of the Thames, see the distant, smoky gas lamp haze of London, and the parliament buildings that stretched beyond.

A few moments later, she dared to reopen the door, then staggered against the wall in relief as she felt the familiar feel of Hus beneath her touch.

She was back.

Back in her own time.

Before she had a moment to think about what had happened, she was faced with a more immediate problem.

Arthur.

"WHERE HAVE YOU BEEN?" he roared.

His expression was wild with fear and worry and it was clear he had been waiting for her.

She cringed. She wasn't the only one. The Boots cowered behind her.

"Well, see..." she tried, wondering how on earth she was supposed to explain what had happened. As it turned out, Arthur wasn't ready to hear it. Not until he'd given her a thorough talking-to.

She followed after him as he marched to the library. His irises whirled, his nostrils began to steam.

"*Don't worry, Arthur,*" he muttered in a strange high pitch that she realized was meant to be an imitation of her voice. "*There's no need for you to come with me, I'll only be a minute, you go on up to bed*," he continued, turning emerald green. "IT'S BEEN OVER AN HOUR! I've been flying all over London trying to find you!"

The Boots jumped in fright. Behind Arthur it looked like most of the library was leaning away from him too. She caught sight of the coat rack, which looked distinctly guilty.

Eglantine grimaced. "I'm sorry, Arthur. But it wasn't my fault. See, what happened was, Hus sneezed again—"

"What?" he said, frowning, and taking a break from shouting, which Eglantine was grateful for. "But I felt nothing here," he continued, clearly confused. Which was surprising as Hus's sneezes *always* left havoc in their wake.

Eglantine knitted her brows in thought. "Maybe it's because the sneeze was felt somewhere else. Or some *time* else, I should say."

"I don't follow."

Eglantine explained what had happened.

Fifteen minutes later the wyvern-butler had turned a very sickly shade of green and was pacing the library, talons on his head in his agitation.

"Hus took you *BACK IN TIME*?" exclaimed Arthur again, as he had done regularly over the past few minutes.

"Yes," said Eglantine, coming in from the kitchen, where she had gone to make him a calming cup of tea. Not that she was feeling all that calm herself. *Why had Hus taken her back in time? What if it happened again? What if she couldn't get back?* But as

Arthur was clearly upset it had oddly taken her mind off her own fears about this new side effect of Hus's cold. "Maybe you should try some tea?" she suggested.

"I'm too wound up to drink tea!" he exclaimed. But he took a sip anyway.

"Okay," he said, breathing deeply. Then, shooting her a look of concern, "Tell me again."

So, she did. She told him how she'd seen her uncle as a boy, and how he'd been acting suspiciously, reading a book it was clear he shouldn't.

He blinked. "I can't remember ever seeing Lichen reading," he said. "Not for enjoyment. He was more the sort of boy who found entertainment from other things – like putting spiders in people's beds…"

Eglantine snorted. That she could very well believe.

"Whatever he was reading upset Mum, well, young Mum."

"That doesn't surprise me. They were often bickering."

Eglantine nodded. She frowned as she remembered the look her mother had given her when she had thought she was in cahoots with Lichen over something.

It had not been pleasant. Her throat grew tight. "Do you think it will happen again – Hus taking us back in time?"

Arthur looked worried. "I really hope not."

So did she.

It was horrible having her mother not know who she was. And the fear that she might get stuck there had been terrifying.

It was well after midnight now, but they both knew there

would be little sleep for them that night.

All Eglantine could think of was the cod-liver-equivalent spell she needed to make for Hus. She had to find a healing one *that would* work. So that whatever mad glitch it was that had sent her back in time *never* happened again.

5

THE IRON PIN AND THE DOLL CUPBOARD

Meanwhile, in Kensington Palace several hours earlier, Victoria was facing a crisis of her own.

She shut her bedroom door and leaned against it in the hope that, for once in her life, her mother would actually leave her alone.

This was wishful thinking, as she soon felt the door being pushed open from the other side and she stumbled forward and almost fell.

"What are you doing, leaning against the door?" cried her mother in outrage. "We were *not* done, Victoria! I would still like to know HOW you got outside the palace and where you went. As would the entire royal guard and Sir Conroy. All the servants have been rounded up. Anyone found to have helped you will be immediately dismissed."

Victoria felt her blood run cold. Eoin could lose his job if they found out that he helped her leave the palace in order to attend the weekly society meeting.

It was awful, because up until a few minutes ago everything had been going so well. Her time-suspension magic had stayed in place the entire duration she was away. When she'd snuck back inside the palace in disguise (Eoin's spare uniform – from a distance she resembled a carriage boy) she'd found everything exactly as she had left it.

Her mother was sitting next to Sir Conroy, frozen in time at the breakfast table, across from what was now ice-cold tea and toast.

The staff, likewise, resembled living paintings, fixed in their various acts of work. One was dusting a chandelier, another was carrying a picture frame down the stairs (presumably to repair it), and the royal guard, who were the only people permitted to use magic near the royals, were frozen outside the palace walls, during their regular morning boundary inspections.

She was feeling pretty smug about her success, until she caught sight of the food and her stomach grumbled audibly and she remembered she had skipped breakfast…

Which was when her magic slipped, and her mother had looked up and seen her dressed like a servant, coming in through the door that led into the garden.

She'd tried to rewind time – but nothing happened. Her magic wouldn't *work*.

She'd tried again and again, clenching and unclenching her

hands, while everyone around her looked at her in shock.

"WHAT ARE YOU DOING?" her mother demanded, standing up so fast she overturned her chair.

Victoria paled, staring at her mother wordlessly, her mouth opening and closing like a fish.

She couldn't believe it. Her magic hadn't failed her like this in a long time. Not since Eglantine had helped her gain control of her Witchspark last year. Since then she'd come to rely on her magic, confident in it in a way she hadn't been before, and she wasn't at all prepared for this *disaster*.

So, she did the only thing she could think of: she turned and ran out of the room.

Unfortunately, her mother followed, hot on her heels, jumping to (some) of the right conclusions for once.

Now, her mother's eyes bore into hers, drilling for truth.

"Victoria, I want an answer! And can you please stop throwing your arms up like that?"

Victoria put her arms down uselessly. She had been trying to use her magic again and failing. Now she needed something, *anything*, that would get her out of this mess...

Her eyes scanned the room and she saw on her dresser a playbill, from a theatre production that she and her governess, Lehzen, had seen the week before. Inspiration struck.

She forced a fake, wide grin and put her (slightly shaking) hands on her hips. "So, you believed it, then – that I was some runaway?"

Her mother took a step back, a look of confusion on her face.

"Well – *yes*?"

Victoria forced a delighted chuckle, then clasped her hands together in apparent relish. "Oh, that's marvellous! See, I was being Viola, from *The Tempest*. Who dresses up as a boy and runs away... you know how sometimes Lehzen and I put on our own plays? I thought I'd see if I could pass as a..." she thought wildly, "runaway myself. I wanted to see if you'd believe me, and...you *did!*"

Her mother blinked in shock.

"You did it to fool me? You wanted me to believe that you'd actually run away from me? I find that a bit hurtful, actually."

Guilt pricked at Victoria's consciousness. *Why did I say runaway?* She didn't want to hurt her mother. "I'm sorry, that wasn't my intention. It was...meant to be a bit of fun."

Her mother frowned. "Where did you get the clothes?"

"I gave them to her," said a voice from behind them.

They both startled.

It was Lehzen, her governess.

Victoria looked at her with startled eyes.

To her shock, Lehzen smiled. "So, she had you fooled, Your Grace? Very naughty," she said with a wink.

Her mother clutched at her chest. "You're saying it's true? This was a...ruse?"

Her mother looked sharply at them both, her head swinging back and forth. Victoria held her breath – would she accept her story or not?

"Very entertaining. Perhaps too much so, Victoria, and for everyone's peace of mind, best not repeated."

"Yes," said Victoria mildly.

Her mother turned to Lehzen. "Victoria, is, of course, still a child, and so these antics are to be expected, but, Lehzen, I would have thought better of you."

"My apologies, Your Grace."

Once her mother had left, Victoria felt the weight of Lehzen's gaze on her, and her knees wobbled slightly in fear.

"Are you going to tell me the truth, or shall I also be made to endure another ridiculous explanation? Where were you?" hissed her governess, her voice stern. "I want the truth."

Victoria nodded, and so she told the truth, though something true that had happened long ago.

"I stole clothes from the laundry room, and snuck out for a walk in the park."

Several expressions crossed over Lehzen's face, from fear to frustration to pity, but the one that held, was resignation. Her eyes softened.

"Victoria, I know it's difficult, this life. We try to make the best of it, you and I, don't we? It's not easy never having much freedom. But you can't take risks like that – you heard your mother. People could get into serious trouble, jobs could be lost – like your friend."

Victoria's eyes widened. "My friend?" she asked, her throat constricting in sudden fear. Did Lehzen know about Eoin? How?

The older woman's expression turned shrewd. "*Yes*, I know you and the carriage boy are friends. I have caught the looks you give each other, and seen him lingering in places he shouldn't to talk with you.

"I know it's hard with no one your own age around, so I haven't tried to put a stop to it. Or felt the need to tell anyone about it. But my responsibility is to your safety, first of all, and if he places you in danger, well, I will be forced to say something. So, think of that," she said, placing a gentle hand on her shoulder, "the next time you consider doing something like this."

Victoria bit her lip, then nodded.

Lehzen had no idea.

The risk was all she thought about.

After the Great Quake, when isle-spark magic was released transforming the United Kingdom into the Magic Isles, one of the first ruling kings used his magic to control people ruthlessly. When he was finally deposed, parliament passed a law that forbade royals from having magic. They figured that monarchs were powerful enough without adding magic to the equation.

For years, this wasn't a concern for Victoria, until she developed powers – the first royal in a century to do so.

For the past year, she feared getting caught with magic, just as much as she feared Eoin getting into trouble for helping her. They'd even had a close shave with the head of the royal guard, Kang Mal-Chin, who'd caught Eoin messing with one of the magic sensors which kept going off around Victoria's secret powers. If she hadn't used her Witchspark to rewind time, Eoin could have faced serious repercussions. Sometimes she still had nightmares about that.

He was the first friend she'd ever had, and the thought of how dangerous it was for him was never out of her mind.

For a while she'd been worried that Eglantine's Uncle Lichen would expose her secret. He knew the truth about her powers. He had seen her use them to help Eglantine fight him off.

But he hadn't said anything yet.

A few months ago, they'd figured out why Lichen might have kept quiet. Only the Whistlewitch had been incarcerated for her crimes against Eglantine's family. She had been charged with kidnap and attempted theft of an important magical home.

Lichen had foisted off all the blame for what he'd done onto the Whistlewitch, denying any involvement. Despite the fact that there had been many witnesses, Lichen maintained that he had been forced to act against his will, and had no recollection of what had happened. He said the Whistlewitch had used an illegal form of magic that made him a kind of puppet, unaware of his actions.

As the Whistlewitch had done this before (to Eglantine's father when she tricked him into signing over his guardianship of the house), it had been difficult to prove otherwise.

Victoria and Eglantine had speculated that Lichen was keeping Victoria's magic secret because he couldn't reveal how he knew about it when he was supposed to have been unaware of anything he was doing.

But that didn't stop Victoria from worrying that he would find a way to tell someone about her powers, especially if there was something he could gain from doing so.

She sighed as she sat on the bed and put her face in her hands. It had been a long day, a long year really, of trying to conceal a part of herself. Of worrying about the price Eoin paid to be her friend. Waiting to be found out.

One day she knew she would have to make a choice: tell the truth about her powers or put her magic away for good so that she could become queen. Some days she leaned more one way than the other. But why did she have to choose at all? Why was it illegal for royals to have magic, but not anybody else? Just because one king, a long time ago, abused his powers didn't mean *she* would. Plenty of other people had magic and power and misused it – just look at the corrupt people in power in the Department... but no one spoke of banning those in government from having magic. Why couldn't the queen of the *Magic Isles* of all places have magic?

She didn't notice when the matchstick-sized iron pin from the portal hopped out of her hair and landed silently on her nightstand. It seemed to regard her with some concern, before it concealed itself behind a tissue box.

Later that afternoon, Victoria found out why her magic had failed.

She was called to the library, along with the rest of the family, by the head of the royal guard, Kang Mal-Chin.

"This morning, after our usual ground inspection, we installed a new spark product – it's something the Department have authorized for high-security areas like the palace, called an Eclipse. It completely prevents magic in action."

"What do you mean?" asked Sir Conroy, confused.

The guard continued: "It will block the magic of anyone who is spark-touched, like us," he pointed at himself, and the rest of the guard. "Our spark sensors and wards prevent outsiders with magic from entering. But, despite these measures, someone spark-touched was detected near the family—"

"Yes, I recall," huffed Conroy. "Like I said, it was likely some faulty spark product that set off the sensors. Or one of you. I mean, how sophisticated are these products?" he said, waggling his fingers at the royal guard.

"They are highly sophisticated – and can certainly tell the difference between magical objects, and people with magic in their veins."

"Doubtful, or they wouldn't have gone off. I still cannot believe we were all subject to a second magic test! I felt like my honour was being questioned," huffed Conroy.

The royal guard frowned. For a moment, Victoria wondered if he was also questioning if Conroy *had* any honour, like she was...

"Nevertheless, if someone tries to conceal a magical power, Eclipse will make it redundant," said Kang Mal-Chin, glancing at Victoria for a beat longer than was entirely comfortable.

She stared at him in mute shock. Did this mean she wouldn't be able to use her powers at the palace any more? Her heart thundered in her ears.

"Well, that sounds good," said Conroy, unaware that Victoria's world was falling apart. "I'm all for increasing our security measures. I was saying only last week that—"

The Duchess interrupted. "But what about our spark products? I don't want to go back to living with candle wax everywhere, not to mention having to give up my spark-phonograph player, just because of some imaginary threat as a result of a faulty spark sensor!"

"No fear of that," mollified the royal guard. "The spark products will still work. The Eclipse is specifically designed to neutralize humans with magic. It won't work on magical beasts, but our wards in the grounds take care of them, so all bases are covered."

"Oh, that's good," said the Duchess, relieved.

"B-but what about you – and the other guards?" asked Victoria, her palms sweaty as she tried to find a way around this disaster. She tried her best to act calm, but it was hard. "W-won't it neutralize your magic too?"

The head of the royal guards, dipped his head in agreement. "Yes, when we are within the palace walls we will not be able to use our abilities – we will only be able to use our powers a few metres from the main building. But if you are concerned for your safety, don't be. We have taken other steps in order to be able to protect you," he said. He shifted lightly so that they could see the sword, hanging by a sheath at his side.

Last year this news – that her magic was effectively blocked – would have been welcomed; it was all Victoria had wanted. A way out of her mess. But now magic had given her so much – freedom, friendship and purpose. To have that taken away, it felt like her world had caved in.

How would she ever be able to leave the palace? How would she ever see her friends again?

While everyone congratulated the guards, Victoria sat silently, and felt her heart sink further and further.

I will not cry, she told herself.

She doubted even Miss Hegotty would have a way around the Eclipse device.

It was well past midnight, and Victoria was listening to her mother snoring in the bed opposite hers.

Sharing a room was part of the oppressive "Kensington System" her mother and Sir Conroy had devised.

Sometimes Victoria woke up to find her mother holding up a mirror beneath her nostrils to make sure that she was still *breathing*.

It all just made her want to scream. Discovering her magic had allowed her to have freedom for the first time in her life. The thought of having to go back to her old life, without magic, was devastating.

Victoria surreptitiously blew her nose on a handkerchief. She despised self-pity but she was giving into it all the same. And right when she was knee-deep in a wave of morose thoughts, a sound distracted her. A rather *annoying* sound. Like a fingernail tapping against wood.

Probably her mother's foot twitching against the bed frame, she mused.

She lay back against the pillows and tried to think about something less gloomy than never getting out of the palace again, or never seeing Huswyvern and her friends, but the tapping sound was making it hard to think positively.

At least her magic would still work in the palace grounds, like it did for the guards, so when they were in the gardens she would have some measure of freedom in summer…but that seemed like a long way away. She sighed.

The faint tapping intensified.

Victoria sat up in irritation, looking across at her mother's bed, which was bathed in a slant of moonlight from an open curtain. Her mother was sleeping peacefully. The tapping noise wasn't coming from her.

Victoria frowned, then scanned the rest of the room.

The sound was coming from her bedside table.

What is that? she thought, staring at something that glowed faintly, while it hopped up and down.

It was an iron pin about the size of a matchstick.

As she stared, it did a little bow.

Did that just happen? Was she dreaming?

The iron pin curved like an arm and beckoned for her to follow. Then it jumped on the floor, and appeared to wait for her.

Victoria hesitated for just a moment.

This wasn't the sort of magic they had in the palace… It was like the pin had come to *life*.

Here there were spark products that had been heavily tested – lights, carriages, clocks and music boxes that were enchanted, yes, but only to do what they had been designed to do. She had only ever seen magic like *this* in one place, where things seemed to move around with a mind of their own.

Huswyvern.

She frowned as she followed the glowing pin, tiptoeing until she was out of her room and in the sitting room next door, where she kept her doll cupboard.

The pin seemed to be on a mission. She watched as it hopped the distance to the closed doll cupboard and then jumped up towards the keyhole.

As she watched, the top of the glowing pin grew and changed before her eyes into the shape of an old gothic house.

Turning from a matchstick pin...into a *key.*

Victoria felt her heart thrum, but this time it wasn't in fear. It was excitement. Hope.

She bit her lip, looked over her shoulder, then turned the key in what was once the cupboard keyhole. There was a faint rattling sound, and the cupboard seemed to light up from within. Victoria opened the door, and gasped.

What she saw wasn't the inside of the cupboard at all, with its shelves full of dolls, but a doorway that led into the parlour of Huswyvern.

6
THE MIDNIGHT VISITOR

The coat rack appeared to be standing in wait, as Victoria stepped through what she realized was a portal.

Her portal.

The coat rack bowed formally, then made to close the door behind her.

It gestured to the space where the cupboard had been, which was now a blank wall. Well, a mostly blank wall – apart from an iron key sitting in a keyhole.

Victoria stared at the coat rack in confusion.

It made a twisting gesture with its arm, and Victoria guessed: "You want me to lock it?"

The coat rack nodded.

Victoria did as instructed, then watched in amazement as the key jumped down from the wall and made its way up her body. She felt it come to a halt in her hair.

"Um – were you...expecting me?" she asked the coat rack.

At her feet, a small footstool swayed like a dog wagging its tail. She took that as a yes.

From his carving on the panelling, Sorcerer Nelson doffed his tricorn hat in greeting.

Victoria didn't share the bond Eglantine did with the house. But she knew in her heart what had happened – Hus had listened to her concerns at their last meeting. "Did you make this portal, just for me? Because of what Eglantine said about how tricky it is for me to get here?'

The coat rack shrugged as if it was nothing.

Victoria felt her throat constrict with tears. The good sort.

It was one of the sweetest things anyone had ever done for her, and she felt immeasurably touched.

"But how? There is a new device at the palace that blocks all magic, how were you able to do it?" asked Victoria.

Sorcerer Nelson was the one who answered.

"It must not block all magic. Perhaps only the kind they thought of as their biggest threat. Human magic, I suppose?"

Victoria gaped at him. "You're right." They had been worried that someone in the palace had magic, someone they couldn't find. She recalled the head of the royal guard saying something about the Eclipse neutralizing magic in *humans*...

If it hadn't been for Hus, she would never have been able to leave the palace.

Victoria felt overcome with emotion. "Thank you, Hus, you are a true friend," she said in a choked voice. "I can't tell you how much it means," and then to her absolute horror and embarrassment, after a very long and tiring day, she burst into tears.

While Hus could, and often did, provide a willing ear, it knew that when intense emotions were involved there was someone else who was far better at that sort of thing.

Which is why it promptly shook Eglantine's bed until she fell out of it into a heap onto the floor.

"Wh-what is it? Is it morning already?" asked Eglantine, opening one bleary eye to check the time. As she awoke she became aware that her nose felt stuffy and her little arm was oddly stiff and tender. Her cold was getting worse. The clock on the mantelpiece glowed in her tower room, where autumn leaves were falling. It was always autumn in Eglantine's room, when it wasn't spring.

She was used to being shaken awake by her magical house so she wouldn't be late for her school lessons with Arthur, but this was something else. She could feel it.

"Is something wrong?"

After the latest glitch with the London portal, she felt a flicker of dread.

Eglantine put her gown on, which rubbed against the itchy spot on her neck and she absently scratched at it. It felt dry and ashy.

"Is it Lichen?" she asked Hus in trepidation, pausing in the hallway by the double staircase. "Please don't tell me we've gone back in time again?"

The row of Saxon masks shook their heads.

She breathed a sigh of relief.

Shortly afterwards, she heard excited stomping coming up the stairs, then saw the shadow of a small dragon-like creature coming nearer as Arthur came flying up, followed closely by The Boots.

Sometimes if Hus couldn't get her out of bed it sent reinforcements.

"Hus woke you too?"

Arthur nodded. "I hope it's not the Vikings again. I'm still recovering from the time they tried to conquer the kitchen."

"Oh, gosh, me too."

The Viking ghosts were confined to the dining room, but sometimes they *did* try and take over other parts of the house. In their latest raiding party, they'd made the mistake of trying to seize the kitchen, though Tidbit the bread gnome had made short shrift of the Norsemen who dared to enter her domain.

Hus led them to the kitchen, where they found something almost as surprising as a Viking invasion.

It was Princess Victoria.

She was sitting in her pyjamas at the scrubbed wooden table, with a steaming mug of cocoa cupped in her hands, and it was clear from her red-rimmed eyes that she had been crying.

Perhaps even more surprising was who they saw sitting next

to her, looking rather awkward. It was Tidbit, who didn't often venture out of her bread cupboard (unless it was to defend it from an invading horde).

"Oh, thank heavens," breathed the gnome when she saw them. She sneezed. Then blew her nose. "This is *not* my department. Begging your pardon, Your Bigness. I'll be off, curlers in me hair, biccies ter get on with, not feeling me best, yer understand," she said. Then she scurried back to her cupboard, where they heard the sound of an iron latch fastening into place, followed by a faint sigh of relief.

It was safe to say that Tidbit was not a people person. (Or a wyvern person or gnome person or any other sort of person person, for that matter.)

Victoria watched the departing gnome in astonishment while Eglantine rushed over to her friend in concern. "Are you okay? What's happened?" She knew it had to be bad if Victoria had risked coming here so late at night.

Arthur took the seat opposite. His eyes were full of worry for the princess as well.

Victoria gave them a brave smile, but it was clear that she had been very upset by something. "I am okay now, thanks to Hus."

They goggled at her.

"What do you mean?" asked Arthur.

"Well, Hus must have heard us earlier when we were speaking about how hard it is for me to get here," she said, and then explained about the portal inside her doll cupboard.

"It made you your own portal?" gasped Eglantine in

amazement. Arthur looked floored. The coat rack nodded, pleased with itself.

"Yes," said Victoria softly, and Eglantine felt tears smart in her eyes when she saw that the other girl was struggling to hold back her own tears.

She reached over and squeezed Victoria's hand.

Eglantine was grateful to Hus for showing her friend such kindness, but she couldn't help feeling a little *worried*. From the way Arthur looked at her with wide eyes, it was clear he was likewise concerned.

Only a few hours ago Huswyvern had suffered an odd side effect from its cold that made Eglantine travel back in *time*. It seemed strange that it would then go and make a new portal, at a time when it knew its magic was misfiring. Especially if that meant putting someone at risk, someone it seemed to hold affection for, if it was making Victoria her own portal.

"And, you know, it couldn't have come at a better time," continued Victoria, not noticing their worry. She explained how the head of the royal guard had introduced a new spark-powered product that made it impossible for her to use her powers at the palace.

"I was lying in bed, wondering how I would *ever* be able to see any of you ever again without my magic, when Huswyvern showed me another way. It's perfect. I often used to sit in my doll cupboard with the door closed. It's the one place where my mother and Lehzen leave me be. It's like Hus knew that, somehow. Like it was waiting for the right moment to create it too, when I was sure all hope was lost."

Eglantine was horrified at everything her friend had endured since she'd last seen her. "I'm so sorry you've been through all that."

Arthur stood and went to the tea station, where he began to rattle the cups rather angrily. "I think we need some calming cocoa," he said, smoke curling from his nostrils. "I thought, when I heard about the Kensington System, that was bad enough, but now this *device* – it's like they've turned the palace into a prison. It's such a stupid rule that royals can't have magic. Outdated and downright unfair."

"I agree," huffed Eglantine. "Why shouldn't the future queen have magic? We're literally called the Magic Isles!"

Victoria gave a wobbly sort of smile. "You know, I was thinking the same thing earlier. Thank you, both. I was feeling so alone, and now – thanks to Hus, and you, well…" she said, and she began to sniffle again.

"I'm glad," said Eglantine, looking at her friend fondly, as Arthur rushed over to give the princess a clean handkerchief.

Eglantine patted the arm of her chair, feeling a surge of love for her home. Even when it was going through its own troubles, Huswyvern would never hesitate to help a friend.

Arthur brought over the cocoa he'd made to the table and inclined his head. "I think Hus must have decided to make a portal, despite the risk."

Victoria raised a brow. "You mean because of its cold? So the portal might not be safe if it sneezes?" she guessed.

Eglantine nodded.

"That did cross my mind," admitted Victoria. "But in my case, considering how impossible it is now to get here without it, I'm willing to take the risk."

Eglantine could understand that. "Hus probably thought you would feel that way. Also, if what happened to me happened to you, maybe with your time-based powers you'd have been able to control things and wouldn't have got stuck like I did," she mused aloud, deep in thought.

Victoria looked confused. "Stuck? What do you mean, stuck?"

Eglantine told her what had happened.

"It took you back in time?" she cried. "To when?"

"About twenty years ago, when Lichen was a boy, and my mother was young too."

"You saw them?" gasped Victoria.

Eglantine pulled a face. "Yes, and let's just say Lichen was still very much Lichen."

"Ugh," said Arthur. "Yes, I recall." The wyvern had been around for over a hundred years and had seen several generations of her family live in this house.

"What happened while you were there?" asked Victoria. "How did you get back?"

"I spotted Lichen hiding by the window seat, reading something he shouldn't. Or at least that's the way my mother made it sound, like he'd stolen a book or something, and was thinking of selling it to someone – she took me for a stranger."

Victoria winced in sympathy. Then frowned. "He was hiding a book – what was it?" she asked.

"I have no idea. I couldn't see. Next thing I knew the world started to spin again and I was back home – and having to deal with Arthur who was—"

"Beside myself!" he admitted. "You *were* gone for an hour."

Victoria's eyes bulged. "That must have been so scary. For both of you."

They nodded.

"It was a bit. But, to be fair, while Hus does lose control when it sneezes, it always puts things right quick enough," said Eglantine. Beneath her feet, she felt a thrum in response.

Victoria agreed. "I'm happy to put up with some glitchy magic if it means I still get to see you all."

Eglantine nodded. "Me too. It's so nice having you here in our pyjamas," she said with a grin. "It's a bit like having a sleepover party, which I've never done with anyone alive before," she said, thinking of the bloodthirsty Viking ghosts or the departed members of her family who liked to visit on All Hallows' Eve.

Victoria had learned to take bizarre comments like this from Eglantine (who had grown up in this weird magical home) in her stride.

"Until Eoin, I'd never had a friend before," said Victoria.

Eglantine never knew what to say when Victoria said things like that. It was odd to feel sorry for a princess, but when you knew her, you didn't really envy her.

"Well, now you have us," she said.

Arthur nodded. "For better or worse." And Victoria beamed as they all chuckled.

Suddenly the bread gnome's cupboard opened, followed by a warm chocolate-scented cloud of steam as the aroma of freshly baked biscuits wafted over, making Eglantine close her eyes in bliss. "Oooh, she's made the good biscuits."

Arthur sprung up to fetch them. "Thank you, Tidbit," he said.

"'Tis not fer you," she said, as she gave him the plate. "'Tis fer Her Most Humongousness." Then she closed her cupboard door with a bang.

Eglantine looked at Arthur and Victoria and stifled a laugh.

"I think she means *Your Highness*."

"I prefer her version," said Victoria, taking a bite. "Next to her I am pretty humongous," she said with a grin. "Which makes a nice change, as I am rather short compared to most."

They all laughed.

Victoria looked at the closed cupboard affectionately. "Jayne is so lovely, honestly. You're so lucky to have her. I hope her cold improves."

"Jayne?" asked Eglantine and Arthur at the same time, a puzzled look on their faces.

"Mrs Jayne Tidbit?" said Victoria. "My mistake, perhaps you call her Mrs Tidbit?"

"Um," said Eglantine. "Generally just Tidbit." *Mrs Tidbit*, she mouthed to Arthur, who looked just as floored.

Which was how they both discovered, after having known the bread gnome for most of their combined lives, that she had a first name.

And, supposedly, at one point, was married?

They ate the biscuits and spoke for several hours. Victoria helped Eglantine gather more ingredients for their next spell to treat Hus's cold. They all agreed that the sooner they cured Hus the better.

"Perhaps I could come back and help you this week?" she asked. "If...if you'd like?"

"That would be wonderful," said Eglantine, who meant it.

Victoria grinned, then snorted. "Just wait till I tell Eoin about the portal. He'll be sad he missed it."

"Bring him next time," said Eglantine, following the princess as she made her way to the parlour where the new portal was.

"I will – and thank you again," Victoria said, and to Hus in particular, giving the wall an affectionate pat, before she took the iron pin from her hair, which changed once more into a key that she placed inside the keyhole in the wall and turned. The wall transformed into a cupboard with shelves upon shelves of dolls, then Victoria stepped inside and disappeared, leaving only a blank wall behind.

7
Burn After Reading

Dear Eglantine and Arthur,

BAR (Burn After Reading!)

The first week of our undercover mission at the Isle-Spark Magical Testing Centre has gone well.

Mum has settled into her new post as an administrator. Her disguise makes her look much like one of my old headmistresses, who was very prim and strict. (I'm sure that was the inspiration!)

Her job is to oversee the daily list of children having their magic tested – making it easy for me to slip in without anyone realizing I shouldn't be there.

My task has been to show up as a different child every day and take the magic test (which, as you know from your own test, is just them passing a metal stick, called a spark-staff, over you while they read your isle-spark magic levels.)

I've taken to haunting the local school to find children who I can turn into for the day. I hope none of the instructors ever recognize them...

So far, nothing strange has happened. Every test I've done shows that I have magic, but it's clear, even just from watching all the kids go in and out, that very few girls are found to have magic, while most wealthy boys do.

Suspicious, right?!

I've only been shapeshifting into boys this past week, on Miss H's orders, but from next week she wants me to switch to girls, so we'll see if that changes anything.

Speaking of Miss H, it is difficult to remember when seeing the sweet little old tea lady doing the rounds with her trolley, with her rosy cheeks and white hair, who calls everyone "dearie" is actually Miss Hegotty! It's SUCH a clever disguise. All the testing instructors love her, and tell her everything, like how long their breaks are, when the Department inspections are – so we're getting a good sense of how the testing centre works, but I don't need to tell you what a genius she is.

But with so much going on, it's no wonder, I suppose, that our next secret society meeting is going to be postponed for a while. Miss H said she would send everyone a letter to let them know (so hopefully you got that before mine). She said we will have to keep at this a while, until we figure out how they are binding children's magic.

At first, I did wonder why Miss H was so sure that they are binding children's magic at testing centres. I mean, it could be happening anywhere...but I see now why she thinks it's here.

I can't explain it exactly, but many of the kids who come out of the centres look a bit different from when they first go in. At first I thought it was disappointment but it's something else. It's like they are a bit washed-out.

Obviously, I can't prove it but I'm sure it's because their powers have been bound. Miss H agrees. So hopefully soon we'll find out how they're doing it.

Just thought I'd send you a letter to let you know what's been happening. Also, to ask if Hus is getting better?

Mum sends her love, as do I.

Nandi

While Eglantine enjoyed Nandi's letter and felt her heart pound with excitement at the thought that Miss Hegotty's suspicions might be correct, she couldn't help feeling left out of such an important and exciting mission.

The fact that the weekly society meetings would be cancelled for a while only made those feelings worse.

She tried to remind herself that it was important the society got to the bottom of any wrongdoing at the Department, but she couldn't help wishing she was a part of the mission too.

From the way everything inside headquarters appeared to be sulking, the chairs sagging, the floor sighing, and the spark-typewriter occasionally clacking a key rather listlessly, it was clear that she wasn't the only one feeling that way.

"I mean, surely I could have done something to help," she muttered. "Arthur and I would have been excellent lookouts."

Sorcerer Nelson tutted. "You have your own mission, Lady Eglantine, and that is to restore the health of our good ship. Just remember, while we may have different tasks, we are all part of the same crew."

"I know."

When she showed the letter to Arthur, hoping perhaps he understood how she was feeling, he laid a talon on her shoulder and said, "It's not the same as being there, but it was nice of Nandi to keep us in the loop."

She nodded. It was.

"It's a pity the meetings are going to be postponed. It will be very interesting to see if anything changes next week when Nandi shapeshifts into girls, and if the test shows a negative result or if her magic gets bound."

Eglantine frowned. Something was niggling at her, then she looked back at the letter and realized what it was. "I'm going to write back to Nandi and tell her to pick children from a school that *isn't* close to the testing centre to shapeshift into – I feel like that's an accident waiting to happen."

He winced. "Good idea."

At least, that was one way she could help.

Perhaps Miss Hegotty knew how Eglantine was feeling, because that night, she received a speed-mail letter from her.

Dear Eglantine,

It won't be long until we have a new member of our society. She is soon to finish my correspondence course, and as mentioned at our last meeting, I can feel that this young witch holds part of the key we need.

There is something else. Something we are not seeing as yet, some part of the puzzle that connects everything together. I think the binding of children's magic is only one piece.

What I haven't explained is that you and Arthur are a part of her puzzle, and what I sense is that only when you meet will we start to get a glimpse of what it is we are missing.

I know it must be frustrating not to be part of the undercover mission. I know Nandi has already informed you that the weekly society meetings will be postponed for a while, but just trust that you are where you are meant to be right now.

Sincerely,
Miss Hegotty

Eglantine read Miss Hegotty's words with a frown, feeling the witch had left her with more questions than answers.

She was part of some unknown girl's puzzle?

She stared at the letter and felt her heart pound in a mix of excitement, apprehension and worry.

Until now, the society had been sure that once they proved that the Department were binding children's magic, their mission would be complete.

Miss Hegotty's letter implied there was more they needed to discover in order to prove how corrupt the Department were.

For the first time, Eglantine wondered: if the Department had got away with secretly binding children's magic for so long, what *else* had they done without anyone realizing?

And how did it connect with her and some girl she had never met?

8

THE MIDNIGHT GANG

The cauldron simmered. The clock struck the witching hour and the spell was cast.

Hus, however, was like a child with its mouth pressed firmly shut, refusing to take its medicine.

"Oh, come on, Hus, it's good for you."

The walls shook in denial.

Eglantine sighed. "You wouldn't think sometimes that I'm thirteen and you are a thousand and thirteen," she muttered to her beloved home.

A cushion blew a raspberry at her.

"Lovely, thanks," she muttered.

Victoria and Eoin sniggered, while Arthur tried to placate the house too.

"The sooner you let the spell in, the sooner this will all be over."

There was a deep, bone-rattling sigh from the house, like all its pipes were letting out air at the same time. The sort of sigh that says, *I doubt it*. But it gave in, finally, and let the cod liver oil spell wash over it.

Hus shuddered. Eglantine pulled a sympathetic face. "Well done, Hus. Sorry."

They were all sitting in the library with the open spellbook in front of them. The cauldron was on the wooden floor, beneath the large window that offered a midnight view of the sea and a fog-covered moon in the distance.

Rat Lord Byron stared out of the window in deep, and silent, contemplation, his claw twitching as if he wished for a pen while a poem brewed inside his mind, but all such thoughts were tossed outside of his head when Eoin yawned and reached for another biscuit. Despite fighting off a cold of her own, Tidbit had been baking up a storm the past week, and her latest was a mouth-watering cinnamon and nut combination. Eglantine and Arthur had tried to get the bread gnome to take it easy and rest, but she had only harrumphed at them to "quit yer mollycoddling", and chased them out of her kitchen with a broom.

As they sat in the library now, the Huswyvern Grimoire flipped past the spell they'd just cast, to the page at the back that was mostly torn out.

"When will we know if the spell worked?" asked Eoin, watching the spellbook with a frown.

Arthur stretched his arms, and stifled a yawn of his own. They had been up until the early hours most nights this week getting everything ready and everyone was feeling tired. "I'm not sure. It could be immediate or take a few hours, according to the spell's instructions."

Ever since Hus had created the palace portal, Eglantine and Arthur had seen Victoria and Eoin almost every other night, usually after midnight when Victoria's mother and governess were asleep.

Without being able to freeze those around her in time, it had taken Victoria several failed attempts to even let Eoin know what had happened.

But once she'd managed to get a message that she needed to speak to him urgently, using their secret language (a system of coded signals they'd developed the year before, inspired by the penny dreadful stories Eoin read) they'd used the portal regularly.

On the plus side, visits from the future queen meant Tidbit, or Jayne, as Victoria (and only Victoria) was allowed to call her, now offered a steady supply of what Eglantine called "the posh biscuits", not the usual digestives Tidbit made for the family.

Suddenly, there was a loud foghorn sound. Even from in the attic library they could hear it.

"It's Sorcerer Nelson. He's sounding the alarm. Something's wrong," cried Arthur.

Victoria's chair dumped the future queen unceremoniously onto the wooden floor, which sprung up beneath her feet like a slide. She struggled to stand as she began to slip from the room.

The only way to keep her balance was to run, which she did.

"What – what's going on?" she cried.

"Hus is worried," said Eglantine. "I think it's trying to tell you that you need to get home!"

Eglantine could sense what Hus was feeling, but that didn't mean she always knew *what* it was worried about. In this case, though, she could guess – Victoria was the only one who had been ejected from her chair.

"Oh, no," breathed Victoria.

Panting and red-faced, they tumbled into the parlour, where the keyhole inside Victoria's portal was flashing red.

The iron pin, which nestled in Victoria's hair, sprang free and flew towards the wall which had transformed into a door. Victoria made to open it, Eoin following at her heels.

Instinctively, Eglantine pulled him back. "No, don't!" she cried.

He looked at her in shock. "What? Why? I have to get home too!"

"Not now. Not if someone is there, waiting. You'll get found with her – and that won't be good for either of you."

His eyes widened. "Of course. I wasn't thinking."

Victoria nodded. "I'll come back for you when I can, Eoin," she said.

Eoin waved her away. "No, don't worry about me. I'll get a lightning-carriage back to the palace later. It's easier for me to slip back in that way, but you go now." He gave her a gentle shove towards the door. Victoria opened it and they all saw rows of dolls, and then, spookily, they heard the sound of someone calling, "Victoria? Are you in there? I woke up and found you out of bed. Is everything alright?"

There was a rattle from behind the door, as if someone was about to open the cupboard from the other side.

Victoria paled. "It's Lehzen, my governess," she whispered. "Thanks, Hus, for warning me." She gave them a last goodbye wave, and stepped inside the cupboard, and the portal vanished along with her.

"For a moment I thought we'd been found out!" cried Eoin, sagging against the wall in relief.

"Me too!" said Eglantine. "It's late, so why don't you stay the night? It'll be nice having you sleep over; you can catch a carriage back in the morning."

Eoin yawned, then nodded. "That sounds good."

Eglantine beamed. "You'll get to try your new room finally."

"Oh, um, yes," he said with less enthusiasm than before.

Eglantine's lips twitched as she bit back a laugh, as she had an idea why.

Sometime later, Eoin followed Eglantine a little reluctantly towards the room he'd failed to show the right level of appreciation for, unless yelping counted. He swallowed nervously as he opened the door, ready to face them again, only to blink in shock.

The sketches of giant rats had been replaced with illustrations of cute flying bunnies and soppy-looking fairies. The coat rack waved its arms in a "ta-dah" sort of way, and Eoin seemed like he might pull something as he tried not to laugh. "It's...erm, beautiful," he choked, mindful of not offending Hus again.

"Isn't it just," said Eglantine, biting her lip to stop giggling herself.

There was a snort from the fireplace.

"You did this on purpose," said Eoin, his mouth falling open.

And suddenly they were all laughing. The rugs bouncing up and down as it chuckled.

Just before dawn, Eglantine woke to a chill in the air. She heard the faintest sigh and smelled the scent of peaches and regret. She sat up fast and then turned, heart clamouring in her chest, to find her mother, the ghost of Lady Heliotrope Bury, sitting on the window seat, looking out into the darkness.

Eglantine rushed over. "Mother."

Like Eglantine, her mother had been bonded to Hus, and that connection had survived even her death.

Her mother's ghost turned to look at her, and for a moment Eglantine held her breath. Her mother's ghost often appeared at different ages, and Eglantine never knew which version it would be, or if she would remember Eglantine at all.

Her mother was younger now than when she had died, possibly in her early twenties. Her dark-blue eyes were just like Eglantine's.

"Darling," she said, and Eglantine felt her stomach twist with love mixed with sadness. It was always a joy to see her mother, though it was a bittersweet one, because Eglantine never knew how long she would stay.

Her mother's ghost reached out a spectral hand to Eglantine's cheek. But of course, Eglantine couldn't feel her touch at all. Her mother's face was full of affection, but also worry.

"It's trying to show you. You need to listen."

"What do you mean?" asked Eglantine.

Her mother looked sad. "It's all my fault. I should have destroyed it, not hidden it where it could be found."

"Listen to who? Find what?" Eglantine asked.

But her mother's ghost was fading fast and all Eglantine was left with were unanswered questions.

9
NEWS AND SCANDALS

Eoin left at dawn.

Eglantine, who was feeling tired, and stuffy with a head cold, was about to pop a piece of toast into her mouth, when Arthur flew into the library in a state of anxiety and flung a newspaper right onto her mound of buttered toast.

"Watch it!" she cried.

"Never mind that. Look!" he cried, pointing at the newspaper with a shaking talon, smoke unfurling from his nostrils in his agitation.

Eglantine picked up the partially buttered newspaper with a frown. She turned to read the first article which was titled: *The Embarrassment of the New Prime Minister.*

THE EMBARRASSMENT OF THE NEW PRIME MINISTER, LORD RAGWORT

Many people have embarrassing relations, but it seems the new prime minister's is on a whole other level. It turns out that Lord Ragwort's half-sister is none other than the infamous outlaw-witch Miss Hegotty, whose magical course has been at the top of the Banned Magic List for years.

Miss Hegotty's "wild magic" has proven hard to squash and Ragwort's numerous attempts over the years to put an end to her Correspondence Course have only met with failure.

Eglantine winced as she read. "There are often articles in the papers about Miss Hegotty but this one does seem especially bad... I know it's still a shock that they actually made Lord Ragwort *prime minister* but—'

"Not that one, I meant the other article!" cried Arthur.

"Oh?" Her eye scanned to the one on the right, and she frowned.

CONNECTION BETWEEN EDINBURGH AND WESTMINSTER PALACE FIRES RULED OUT

> After a six-month investigation, the Banned Magic Office has ruled out magic as a cause of the fire at the Palace of Westminster, which resulted in the loss of many Departmental records.
>
> The Office has also ruled out any connection with a fire that burned down the Witch's Cat pub in Edinburgh last year.
>
> The pub owner's daughter claimed that her father's ghost, George Chan, told her both fires were caused by magical interference.
>
> Departmental spokesperson, Edel Scareweed, said: "This is simply not the case. Ghosts, at the end of the day, were once human, and like any human, they get things wrong."

"I suppose it might have been a stretch that the fires were linked. It's also possible that ghosts can be mistaken—" began Eglantine, feeling a pang as she thought of her own ghost mother and her mysterious warning the night before.

Arthur groaned, and put his head in his talons in frustration for a moment. "Not that one either, milady, the one below the one on Lord Ragwort. The one on *Lichen*!"

She gasped, then turned quickly to look. She had completely missed it! Her face turned white as she read, understanding at last what had caused Arthur such distress.

"This can't be happening," she whimpered.

LORD LICHEN BURY TO HEAD BANNED MAGIC OFFICE

Lord Lichen Bury has been promoted to the head of the Banned Magic Office. Some of his critics are surprised at the move, considering that earlier this year Lord Bury was under investigation for his involvement with the infamous Whistlewitch. The sorcerer was charged with kidnapping Lord Bury's brother-in-law and attempted theft of the family's sentient home. Lord Bury denied any involvement, claiming that the Whistlewitch used mind magic to control him.

"Lord Bury was an innocent victim of those crimes. He has proven himself to be someone we can trust, someone who shares the same vision many of us have at the Department for how magic should be managed. He will be a worthy successor," said his predecessor, Prime Minister Ragwort.

Lord Bury said, "I am committed to maintaining the safety of the Isles, and taking a tough stance."

Eglantine stood up, fast. "B-but how is this even possible? How could he have been promoted after everything he did? How could they just believe he had no involvement in the Whistlewitch's crimes? How can they dismiss everything that we said? The Department said it would keep us updated before it concluded its investigation into his involvement."

"Looks like they just did," said Arthur, an angry set to his mouth. Then his eye fell on the paper and steam began to curl from his nostrils. "I hadn't finished the article, I was shocked enough by his appointment, but this..." he said, his voice trailing off. He looked up at her, and the expression in his eyes was a mix of sadness and fury. "This might be one of the reasons he got the job. He's promised to have a harder stance on the 'Magical Creature Problem'."

He looked as if someone had thrown cold water in his face. "I knew he never liked me, but I never imagined he hated my *kind*."

"What?" cried Eglantine, taking the paper and reading on, feeling her own face turn red and blotchy in anger.

> Lord Bury also vowed to come up with a solution to the "Magical Creature Problem" and their "ridiculous demands" once and for all.
>
> Lord Bury was referring to magical creatures and their ongoing campaign for equal rights, which has caused friction in recent months between them and the Department. Now the Department has hit back with a clear refusal.
>
> "Since the Quake, when magical creatures awoke from stone, the Department put in place a

> set of simple rules for these dangerous beasts to follow so that they could live harmoniously with humans. Any demand that these rules be abandoned is not only absurd, but serves as proof that the beasts do not care about the safety of humans at all, which is why we have taken preventative action to ensure the safety of everyone in the Isles."

Eglantine gasped. "He's making it sound as if magical creatures pose a threat to humans."

Arthur nodded. "Yes. He's deliberately misleading people about what we want. Having the same rights isn't about us not following laws! We don't have the vote and our kind does not have a representative in parliament, so none of our concerns are ever heard. Like the fact that we get paid less than humans for doing the same jobs, which is hardly fair. Or we are discriminated against because we are not human. Many landlords refuse to rent to us even if they have the space, not to mention the fact that we constantly find ourselves on the Banned Magic List every time one of us does something wrong, which would never happen with humans. They don't cut the tree down when they find one bad apple when it comes to their own kind."

"You're so right."

Eglantine felt her heart twist for him. She didn't stop him from saying the list's full name, like she normally would, as it always magically appeared when it was spoken aloud.

After a moment, a scroll appeared in mid-air in a puff of smoke and she read it, feeling sick as she realized that the Department's "preventative action" was to take away even more of their rights.

For the first time in years something besides Miss Hegotty's course topped the list and it sent a shiver down Eglantine's spine.

Eglantine felt her stomach drop. "He can't be serious," she whispered.

"What is it?" asked Arthur.

"Magical creatures have been banned from all governmental and civil service positions."

He gasped.

She slapped the list on the table with a thud. "That's discrimination!"

He nodded. "They've always been guilty of that. Like when the king's wyvern-healer gave him goat ointment instead of gout ointment by mistake and wyvern-healers were on the Banned List for a while. But that blew over once the king was back to normal. This feels different."

"Yes."

The idea that Lichen had not only got away with what he'd done to her family, but had been rewarded for it, made her feel terrible. But the fact he had made it his mission to make life impossible for magical creatures like Arthur was even worse. The news cast a heavy shadow over their week.

* * *

As the days passed, Eglantine grew worried about Arthur, who was quiet and withdrawn. Some of the emerald-green scales around his neck had faded to a greyish-khaki colour, and she was concerned that the stress of everything must be affecting him.

The one bright spot had been the latest healing spell. For the past few days there had been no signs of illness at all.

That hope was dashed the very next morning when Hus let out such a powerful sneeze that the east and west wing swapped themselves completely around.

Eglantine woke up when it happened, feeling waves of anxiety coming from Hus. Her heart raced in response, but she didn't notice what was wrong at first.

Not until she got out of bed, rubbing sleep from her eyes and walked straight into a wall that wasn't usually there. She rubbed her forehead in shock. Everything in her room was now on the opposite side to where it usually was, like some kind of weird mirror world.

That was when she saw what had happened. That the two wings of the house had swapped. She could feel Hus's anxiety thrumming through the floor.

She patted the walls soothingly, and watched as several armoured suits rushed from what had been the east wing looking just as confused as she was.

As was the horde of Viking ghosts – although they all cheered thinking they had finally managed to take over more than the dining room.

"Oh, Hus," she said softly. She felt her own chest tighten and she began to cough.

"That doesn't sound good," said Arthur, coming up the stairs, looking worried.

"I'm fine," said Eglantine, waving away his concerns. She was still a bit under the weather but it was nothing compared to Hus.

"I really thought that Hus was better," she said with a sigh.

"Me too," he said, then brightened. "But maybe this will have some answers?" he said, holding up an envelope. "It looks like you've finally got a response from one of the other sentient homes you wrote to."

Eglantine took the letter from him, and felt her spirits rise as she opened it, only for it to come crashing back down a few seconds later.

Dear Lady Eglantine,

I wish I had some better news for you. We are at our wits' end ourselves.

Bal is just not herself. She keeps sneezing and everything is topsy-turvy. Apparently, it's the same at Blarney Castle. Neither of us have a Grimoire like Huswyvern does, so, please, if you find a spell that works, I beg you to pass it on.

Sincerely,
Heather McGowen
Caretaker of Balmoral Castle

By evening, the wings of the house were back to their usual places and Eglantine climbed into bed. She peered at the Grimoire in determination. There were four more healing spells she could try.

"We just need the right one, Hus," she said.

There was a weary sigh from the house and the spellbook flicked its pages towards the end again where there was nothing apart from a tiny scrap of torn paper.

She couldn't help wondering if there was another reason Hus kept showing it to her. Perhaps there had once been a spell there that might have helped?

"Is there a way to get the spell back?" she asked, and the chairs shook their heads.

She frowned. "Well, then, it's no help to us," she said, thinking of the other sentient homes. It was so strange that, like Hus, they were also unwell.

Hopefully one of these healing spells would work and she could send it on to the other homes.

She held on tight, then flicked back towards a promising spell that helped with spasms. "That's sort of like sneezing, right?" she mused aloud. "It doesn't seem that complicated, though it does involve brewing a sticky unguent that we will have to slather onto the walls," she said, pulling a disgusted face. The words "sticky" and "unguent" did not sound pleasant.

Clearly Hus agreed, as the book went flying across the room and closed with a thud. Followed by a shudder from Hus.

She patted the walls. "I don't blame you. But if it will help..."

There was a *harrumph* from the door.

To be fair, Eglantine wasn't feeling all that great herself. She had started to have a dry cough that wouldn't go away. Her little arm felt a bit achy, and the ashy spot on her neck that had been itchy was tender too.

Hus could tell she wasn't feeling great as, about a minute later, a small footstool came rushing inside her room with a honey and lemon tea for her.

She smiled as she took it from the footstool, which wagged in response. "Hus, we look after each other, that's the deal."

She got up to fetch the Grimoire, and climbed back in bed with it, and the tea, which made her feel instantly a bit better, only to find something else waiting for her.

It was a blue envelope.

Another speed-mail letter from Miss Hegotty.

She placed the spellbook down, to Hus's relief, and opened the letter.

Dear Eglantine and Arthur,

The time has come. Our newest society member is about to join us.

As I mentioned in my last letter, she is a piece of the puzzle we need and you are both a part of hers. She is in need of a friend, and she may help you find out how to move forward with Hus.

You will find her in The Dragon Book Apothecary & Coffee Emporium in Edinburgh tomorrow afternoon at one p.m. I would suggest you take a lightning-carriage.

Sincerely,
Miss Hegotty

10

BROKEN DREAMS AND LOST GHOSTS

Twelve-year-old aspiring journalist Myrtle Chan's day turned from bad to worse as the editor of *The Weekly Spellcast* frogmarched her outside and threw her articles into the mud.

"Mr Chatterjee, that was hardly necessary," she gasped, pushing up a pair of gold wire-rimmed glasses onto her small button nose before she bent to pick up the papers, her long, shiny black hair swinging like a curtain over her face.

She dusted off one of the stories she really cared about, and gave him a winning smile.

"You said this one about the mysterious flu affecting magical creatures seemed promising? You said it might be worth looking into, especially as the Department hasn't said anything about it..."

He harrumphed. "That was before you tried to trick me into giving you a job, Miss Chan," he spat, his voice dripping with disdain.

Myrtle stared at him sheepishly. It was true. She'd used an ageing potion so that she could meet the legal age requirement for a junior reporter. But one of the spark sensors he had in his office detected that she had used a potion on herself (the news office used a range of magical detectors to ensure their safety).

"It was more of a white lie…"

His eyes narrowed. "The truth, Miss Chan, does not come in *different colours.*"

Myrtle wasn't so sure. She couldn't help thinking of the one she told her Aunt Ida every time she asked how she was doing since her father's death six months ago, when a fire had burned down his pub, The Witch's Cat. Myrtle always said she was fine.

Telling her aunt that she was still basically holding things together by the skin of her teeth would just make her worry about her even more than she already did.

But she couldn't tell Mr Chatterjee any of that.

"Miss Chan, the fact that you were willing to deceive me in such a way tells me that you don't value the truth, and there is no place for someone on this paper who doesn't."

Myrtle gasped. "I *do* value the truth – that's why I want to be a journalist."

It was her Witchspark. She could sense when someone was telling the truth, and she could even store it in objects, as a kind of audio recording that played back.

She couldn't tell him about that either, as having a Witchspark was banned. A Witchspark was a magical power that was unique to each witch or wizard that had to be unlocked from within. Ordinary witches and wizards in the Magic Isles could perform foundation magic, but the knowledge of how to unlock one's Witchspark was kept a secret.

The Department reserved those skills for a select handful of people they could tell would be useful to them, who were then chosen to become sorcerers at university. (Having a Witchspark was what made one a sorcerer in the first place.) Telling him she had this sort of banned magic would only get her into more trouble.

"Well, you have a funny way of showing it," he continued. "How am I ever supposed to trust you, if the first thing you've shown me about yourself is your ability to lie?"

Myrtle turned pale. Tears of shame pricked at her eyes.

He turned to leave.

"Mr Chatterjee," she called after him, desperate for him to understand. She did want a job, yes, but she also really wanted the paper to look into the story she'd found concerning magical creatures. "If I'd come to you with my story without making myself seem older, you wouldn't have listened to me."

He turned, then frowned. "No, Miss Chan, you only *thought* I wouldn't listen. I wouldn't be a newsman worth my salt if I didn't listen to everyone who had a story to tell. Stories don't have age limits and neither do sources," he said, then turned to leave once more.

Myrtle stared after his retreating back.

"Mr Chatterjee, I'm sorry," she called. "I will find a way to show you that you *can* trust me."

He paused, and then almost reluctantly nodded his head. "I hope so, Miss Chan."

Myrtle stepped dejectedly into the fog-filled streets of Edinburgh. She walked without much thought of where she was going, until she looked up and found herself in front of her father's old pub, The Witch's Cat, and felt her heart sink even further. The sign was blackened from the fire, as was the outside of the building. The windows were still boarded up.

His ghost was there now, standing on the street opposite the pub. Just as it had appeared almost every day since he'd died six months ago.

He was staring at something only he seemed able to see.

"Hello, Father," she said. "I didn't get the job." He didn't recognize her, just stared woodenly past her at his old business.

"I have to warn them," he muttered.

He always said that.

"You did warn the others about the fire, Father. You must have."

No one else had been in the building the night he'd died.

He shook his head vehemently, his dark eyes wild. "The fires are connected. I have to tell them about the Witchlight. Before the planets align."

Myrtle sighed. She'd written to the Department and they had looked into it. The fire here *had* seemed to bear a resemblance to the one that broke out in the Palace of Westminster, but they had found that they weren't connected at all, and no one could tell her what a "Witchlight" was. She'd assumed, at first, that it was something to do with the fire that burned down the pub, but the authorities said the fire was due to a faulty oven and not any kind of enchantment...

"I told the Department, remember? They looked into all of this," said Myrtle in frustration. Wasn't that what one was supposed to do with ghosts – help them with their unfinished business so they could move on? Her father didn't seem able to accept any of it.

"*I have to warn them.*"

"You *did.*"

Up close he was still him. The same lines around his eyes, the same five o'clock shadow. The same curl to the back of his hair which he would play with absently, while he thought of other things.

He looked back at her and for a moment it seemed as if he recognized her. Then his expression went blank and he went back to staring at his pub. The worried look returned.

Myrtle closed her eyes. *I will not cry*, she told herself. Not in front of him.

She'd promised herself she wouldn't get angry with him again either. But that was a promise she failed to keep.

"Why do you keep coming here?" she snapped, hiding her hurt

that he visited his business and not his only child, who missed him so much her heart felt like it might burst. "You got everyone out of that fire except for yourself. If you have to be so worried about something, why can't it be me? Why don't you care that you left me behind?"

Shouting was a mistake.

Ghosts didn't linger when emotions were high.

She saw something flicker across his face, which went from blank to what almost looked pained, before he vanished.

She sighed, and had to breathe through her mouth to calm down.

Not all ghosts were the same. Some came back and seemed to have all their memories, others seemed to lose who they once were. Some came at different ages. Her father haunted his business. It was clear to her that his pub mattered more to him than the daughter he left behind. The fact that he couldn't see how much that hurt her just made her sadder still.

She let out another sigh, then adjusted the portfolio under her arm, and set off for The Dragon Book Apothecary & Coffee Emporium down the street. She couldn't face the thought of going home to her aunt's enquiring eyes, not now.

Just before she turned to open the door, a blue envelope sailed into the air in front of her.

She grabbed it instinctively, only to gasp.

It was addressed to *her*.

Her eyes widened.

It was a letter from Miss Hegotty. A letter that appeared oddly bulky. She opened it and saw a sprig of myrtle that had a faint sheen of enchantment.

Dear Miss Chan,

You have been bold and brave and now it is my pleasure to welcome you to the Secret Society of Witches.

With that in mind, I send you two of my best. I believe there is much you can help each other with and I sense that you each hold part of a puzzle the other needs.

I look forward, in due course, to meeting you in person at headquarters. You will find the portal at the foot of Big Ben.

Miss Hegotty

PS The protection flower in the envelope is enchanted. The others will explain more.

PPS I figured you wouldn't object to your protection flower being your namesake.

11
The Dragon Book Apothecary & Coffee Emporium

The lightning-carriage tore through the countryside, taking Eglantine and Arthur to the city of Edinburgh, at a speed that was not comfortable for those prone to motion sickness, as Eglantine most certainly was.

Under normal circumstances (and using a far slower spark-carriage) Eglantine would have been delighted at the prospect of getting to visit such a beautiful, historic city. But the speed at which they were travelling made it impossible to appreciate any of the scenery that blitzed past the window of the driverless carriage.

A sign above the compartment door made a bold promise.

City to City by Lightning-Carriage!

From London to Edinburgh in twenty minutes flat – or your money back!
A proud innovation of Spark-Travel Inc.

Eglantine (and her stomach) could well believe it.

Arthur meanwhile looked utterly unaffected and had been reading a newspaper throughout their short journey, his pince-nez perched on the bottom of his snout. He looked up in surprise and delight. "Marvellous. We're here already."

Marvellous was not the word Eglantine would have used.

When they came to a stop on a cobbled street, Eglantine needed a full minute to recover before she was able to get on her feet.

"That must be it," she said. She bent over as she took a deep breath, and tried not to heave her lunch, pointing at a sign that featured a dragon curled up on a sofa with a book in its claws.

It read: *The Dragon Book Apothecary & Coffee Emporium.*

The windows were lit with soft amber lights that felt like a beacon guiding them out of the cold.

They opened the door, which tinkled with the sound of a bell. The air inside was thick with the scent of cinnamon, coffee and books. The shop was divided into two, with a cafe on the left, and a bookshop on the right.

"Delicious," said Arthur, closing his eyes to savour the aroma.

A smartly dressed gargoyle was playing a lullaby of sorts on the piano and Eglantine felt herself relax after her harrowing ride.

On the cafe side, they could see a large hearth with a crackling fire and several tartan-and-leather armchairs of various sizes, to accommodate its varying clientele of dragons, gargoyles, gnomes and humans.

On the bookshop side, there was a large black dragon, wearing a pair of gold wire-rimmed spectacles, sitting behind a large, highly polished mahogany desk, a book in his claws. Just like the sign outside. On either side of him were wooden shelves, stacked from floor to ceiling with books. Some of the books were covered with glass bell jars. Eglantine wondered why. Perhaps they contained powerful magic, secrets, or ideas, and needed to be contained in some way? Or perhaps it was just a fun bit of decor. Either way, it added to the charm. On the walls, there were framed prints of book covers as well as sketches of medicinal plants, and the whole thing resembled a kind of apothecary, which Eglantine guessed must be what had inspired part of the store's name.

Two signs on the wall above the mahogany desk read:

A heart-warming drink, a good book and
a comfy chair can solve many ills.
Come in, weary traveller, and stop for a while.

Eglantine and Arthur looked around in awe.

"I think if I could ever get a special portal of my own, I'd like it to come here," whispered Eglantine, catching sight of a gnomish waiter carrying a steaming cauldron of hot chocolate to a red dragon who was knitting in the corner.

Arthur was more focused on the job at wing. "This place is pretty busy. How are we meant to know who we're supposed to meet? I can't believe Miss Hegotty didn't give us a name at all." He looked around anxiously.

Eglantine raised a brow. "Can't you?"

He sighed. Then chuckled slightly. "Good point."

Miss Hegotty was partial to a bit of mystery in her operations.

The clock on the wall by the cafe side said it was 12.50 p.m. "Maybe she described us to the person we're meant to meet?"

"Talons crossed," said Arthur hopefully. "We've got a little bit of time. I suppose it wouldn't hurt to have a browse." Arthur's eyes had lit up at the sight of the books.

Eglantine grinned. "I suppose not."

She loved reading almost as much as the wyvern-butler.

They made their way over to the bookshop side, where Arthur and Eglantine greeted the black dragon.

"You have a beautiful shop," said Eglantine, who half-wished she had two extra pairs of eyes so she could see everything.

"Thank you," said the dragon, with a warm smile from behind the desk. "My name is Knox. You're welcome to browse, but let me know if you'd like me to prescribe you something to read. I have a knack for it, you see."

Arthur looked at the dragon in some surprise. "A book prescription? How does that work?"

The dragon peered at Arthur contemplatively. He had deep gold eyes. "I have a look at you, and after a while I get a sense of what you might need."

Eglantine's eyes widened. "Is it like medicine?"

Knox frowned. "Sometimes it can be healing, yes. But people need all sorts of things – sometimes information, sometimes a bit of comfort or a laugh, sometimes something I can't really understand, I just feel in my bones that they need it."

They stared at him.

"Shall I?" said Knox, holding out a talon towards Eglantine.

Eglantine nodded, and put her hand on the dragon's talon.

He held on rather gently, and then stared deeply into her eyes. It should have been uncomfortable, being stared at like that, but for some reason, it wasn't. She felt safe, and his golden eyes reminded her of the beach sand at home. His irises whirled, and after a while he blinked, like he was coming out of a kind of trance, and let out a small puff of air.

He looked a bit shocked. "I can't believe it."

It was only then that Eglantine began to feel somewhat uncomfortable. "What is it?" she asked.

"Something that's never happened before."

The bell tinkled, and a young girl with black hair and gold-rimmed glasses stepped inside. She had mud on her skirt and she was carrying a satchel that was likewise covered in dirt.

She looked like she had the weight of the world on her shoulders. But as she entered, she took a deep breath of the cinnamon-scented air and a tiny smile flitted on her face, as if she'd entered a kind of refuge.

Knox gasped as he looked from Eglantine to the new customer, his mouth falling open slightly. "Well, now that *is* really interesting.

I was just thinking about you and you appeared, Myrtle!"

"You were?" said the girl, looking surprised.

Knox nodded. "When I did my reading now, for – sorry, how rude of me, what is your name?" the dragon asked.

"Eglantine."

"For Eglantine. The book that came to mind is quite rare and old and long since banned by the Department."

Myrtle frowned. "Okay, I suppose that is interesting...but why did it make you think of me? And why are you telling me about – erm – Eglantine's book prescription? I thought you always keep them private."

"I do, usually, when they only involve one person," said Knox. "But, see, the book Eglantine appears to need is something I had a sense that *you* needed too."

Myrtle and Eglantine looked at each other in shock.

Knox continued, "I have it here," he said, then bent to fetch a book from below the counter. "I must say, this has never happened before – two customers both needing the same book!"

Eglantine's eyes widened. She stepped closer, as Myrtle did the same, to look at the title.

It was called *The Creatures and Houses That Awoke from Stone* by Seraphine Kalk.

Eglantine could tell straight away why Knox might have felt called to prescribe that particular book to her. She hoped it might contain some clue as to what to do when magical homes like Hus got ill...but why did this girl need it? She looked from the dragon to Myrtle. Then she saw a tiny piece of a blue envelope peeping out of the satchel and she gasped in recognition.

"I think I know why this happened," breathed Eglantine. She saw across the way that the clock was now pointing to one o'clock *precisely*.

"You do?" said Arthur.

"Yes," said Eglantine, pointing a finger towards the scrap of blue envelope. Arthur inhaled softly when he saw it. "Why, of course."

Myrtle looked confused. "What do you mean?"

"My name is Eglantine Bury, and this is Arthur. We were sent by a witch who I think you might know, someone who sends speed-mail by a certain blue shade," said Eglantine meaningfully, gesturing at the tip of the envelope. "She sent us to welcome our newest member."

Myrtle's eyes widened. "Oh!" she exclaimed, a smile lighting up her features. "I received her invitation not five minutes ago, as I was on my way here!"

It was their turn to be amazed by the mysterious workings of Miss Hegotty.

Ten minutes later, Eglantine, Myrtle and Arthur were sitting at a table in the cafe near the crackling fire, with steaming mugs of hot chocolate.

As soon as they'd sat down, Arthur looked around, then placed a stone under the table.

"Just popping down a muffle stone," he explained.

Myrtle raised a brow. "Come again?"

"It's a stone that has been enchanted to muffle conversation, so anyone passing our table won't be able to hear what we say. Miss Hegotty uses them whenever we're in public."

"Oh, that's handy," breathed Myrtle, eyes alight. She was soon peppering them with questions about the society, and Miss Hegotty.

"What is she like? I thought she might be scary when I first joined her course, but she isn't, is she? Well, I didn't think so. Did you also join her school first? I couldn't believe it when I heard that almost no one actually goes through with her course, but I suppose that's to be expected considering the fear of being branded –" she whispered it – "*ungovernable*, but I just felt I had to sign up, I *had* to know if I could be a witch. Was your magic bound too?"

Myrtle rattled on, not giving them a second to answer.

"It's crazy speaking about magic so freely. At home, I've had to keep the fact that I have unlocked my magic a secret. My Aunt Ida would be horrified I'd broken the law. She's a stickler for the rules."

Eglantine opened her mouth to answer some of Myrtle's questions and eventually Myrtle realized that she had been having a completely one-sided conversation. She blushed. "Sorry, I'm babbling. It happens when I'm nervous. I'll shut up now," she said, taking a sip of hot chocolate and then spilling some of it down her blouse. "Oh, gosh."

Arthur handed her a handkerchief, and Eglantine performed

a quick spot clean spell she'd learned from the Huswyvern Grimoire.

Eglantine grinned. If she were being honest, there was a part of her that was just so grateful for how normally Myrtle acted around her. She must have noticed that she didn't have two hands, and yet she hadn't even glanced at her little arm. Or asked about it. Eglantine didn't mind answering questions about how she was born, but the truth was, people often forgot to treat her as a person before they launched into questions, and, well, it wasn't like they had a *right* to know, but some people demanded answers as if it were their business, when it really had nothing to do with them. So, this was…refreshing.

"Don't worry, I was exactly the same the first time I met someone who'd done Miss Hegotty's course," said Eglantine with a grin. She couldn't help taking a shine to the girl.

"Really?" said Myrtle, her eyes sparkling.

Eglantine frowned in thought. "Okay, let's answer those questions. Hopefully I remember all of them," she said with a wink. "You asked what Miss Hegotty is like – well, she's everything you expect – but then she surprises you by being really warm and kind and sometimes you forget that she's *that* Miss Hegotty, until, well, you're reminded when she does something like today…"

"Ah, I can see that being true," said Myrtle.

Then Eglantine told her about why she joined Miss Hegotty's course, when her uncle and the Whistlewitch had tried to steal Huswyvern from her.

Myrtle gasped. "Hang on a minute! The Whistlewitch?! I read about that in the papers, gosh! You're *Lady Eglantine Bury*?"

Eglantine nodded.

"Thank goodness the Whistlewitch was locked up." She frowned. "But your uncle wasn't, was he? He's the new Head of the Banned Magic Office... I thought that was fishy."

"Very fishy, trust me," said Eglantine.

Myrtle nodded. Then raised a brow at Arthur meaningfully.

"And even more so with how they're treating magical creatures – I mean, magical creatures have been asking for equal rights when it comes to renting homes or finding work for years, that isn't really new – so why is the Department acting as if magical creatures don't want to follow the law any more? Why are they suddenly telling everyone they're dangerous and preventing them from working in governmental positions? It doesn't make sense."

"You're right," said Arthur. "But, to be fair, none of their actions towards us have ever made much sense."

"That's true."

"Still," said Arthur, "I think you're on to something, their new 'tough stance' on magical creatures feels like it's come out of nowhere."

"I agree. Knox's cafe used to attract more humans. The regulars, who actually know magical creatures like Knox, still come, but I think what the Department have been saying about magical creatures is making people fear them. There must be something more to this. They're trying to keep power to themselves and getting rid of anything that seems like a threat to that – like girls having magic or magical creatures having any control," said Myrtle.

Arthur looked impressed. "Not many people examine the news like you do."

Myrtle nodded, and looked at him seriously. "I have to. I want to be a journalist someday. You know, I thought it might be hard to speak to you both about why I joined Miss Hegotty's course. But I should have realized that the ones who went through with it were like me; they felt they had no other choice."

"Yes," agreed Eglantine.

Myrtle continued. "I did her course partly because I wanted to see if there was any truth to the rumours that something or someone was preventing children from getting their magic. I feel it's important to expose the truth. But the main reason was because my father passed away six months ago."

There was a sharp intake of breath from both Eglantine and Arthur.

"I'm so sorry," breathed Eglantine.

"Thank you. Shortly after he died in a fire, he came back as a ghost. Though he isn't like the ghosts I have read about. He doesn't recognize me. He keeps saying the same thing over and over again. That he wants to warn people about the fire. I thought that maybe if I had magic I could get through to him. Help him to pass over. But nothing I've tried so far has worked."

"Oh, Myrtle," said Eglantine sadly. "I know how hard that can be. My mother visits as a ghost too. Sometimes she doesn't know me either."

Myrtle stared at Eglantine in surprise. "Your mother haunts you?"

"Yes. I might be able to help you get through to him. I have seen a spell that allows you to connect with ghosts in Huswyvern's old spellbook. I can show it to you when you come and visit."

"Really?"

"Of course."

There was a moment when it looked like Myrtle was trying hard not to cry. They both took a sip of their now rather cold hot chocolates.

Arthur picked up the book Knox had prescribed both Eglantine and Myrtle.

The Creatures and Houses That Awoke from Stone by Seraphine Kalk.

"Do you mind if I have a look at this?"

They shook their heads, then looked from him to each other, glad to change the subject and also to finally discuss the book, which had been sitting there like a silent guest neither of them could ignore.

"The thing is," said Eglantine, "I sort of know why Knox might have thought I'd need that book."

"You do?" asked Myrtle.

Eglantine's face looked grave. "Huswyvern is sick, and we've been struggling to find a cure."

Myrtle's mouth popped open in surprise. "Your magical house is *sick*? I didn't know they could get ill."

Eglantine sighed. "Neither did I. I don't remember it ever getting sick before."

"Nor I," said Arthur, paging through the book, his brow furrowed.

Just then Knox walked past and sneezed.

Myrtle frowned as she watched the dragon. "Well, the reason Knox most likely prescribed the book for me is because I came across a story that the Department have been keeping quiet about – a flu that seems to be spreading amongst magical creatures."

"What?" breathed Eglantine in surprise, looking over at Arthur, who hadn't heard, he was too absorbed with whatever he was reading.

Myrtle inclined her head. "My neighbour, Mr Knotweed, told me about it. He's a gargoyle and he said magical creatures never get ill, so he was alarmed to find that he had flu symptoms, along with many of his friends. When he wrote to the Department to let them know what was happening, hoping they'd look into it and try to find out what was causing it, or at least warn other magical creatures about it, he got a response to say that it was nothing to be worried about. That it was just a regular, seasonal flu. Even though none of them had ever experienced that before.

"Then things turned really strange, because the Department finished the letter by telling him he was officially banned from talking about it with other magical creatures as it might cause them to worry unnecessarily. If he did, he would be labelled a Public Nuisance and sent to *prison*."

"What?" cried Eglantine. "Just for talking about it?"

"*I know, right?*"

Arthur looked up from the book and appeared to tune into the conversation again.

"But then last week, we realized the Department must be covering something up, and they were lying when they said it was just a regular, seasonal flu. Because Mr Knotweed's left foot turned to *stone*."

"No!" gasped Eglantine.

Arthur paled. "Whatever it is, it couldn't have been a 'flu' at all," he said, an odd look on his face as he touched his neck where a large patch of his scales had faded to a greyish khaki colour. He appeared worried, and so did Eglantine as she looked at him. "We don't get sick, ever."

Myrtle blinked. "*That's* what Mr Knotweed said too. At first, I thought maybe he was exaggerating, but my Witchspark is the ability to sense the truth, and he was telling me the truth." She looked at Arthur. "Just as you are now."

Arthur gulped. "I think that's why Knox prescribed this book to you both," he said, eyes wide, as he showed them a passage.

For years, people have believed that the blood of a magical creature – or indeed, the stone of a sentient home – may offer healing properties, because none have ever reported experiencing illness of any kind.

> Spark-scientists have long tried to understand why this could be so.
>
> It was for this reason that in the early years after the Quake (which released isle-spark and awakened magical beings from stone), it was legal to hunt magic creatures and take samples from magical homes...

Eglantine breathed in sharply. "They're the same! Magical creatures and homes. So whatever's affecting Mr Knotweed is affecting Huswyvern too."

She looked worriedly at Arthur. "You haven't been yourself either. I thought it was the stress of trying to find a cure for Hus, combined with news about how they are treating magical creatures... Are you okay? How do you feel?"

He frowned. "A bit off," he admitted.

Eglantine swallowed. She thought of Tidbit, who had been fighting off a cold now for weeks. She didn't like this at all. Her heart was beginning to race in fear.

Myrtle frowned.

"But it's like Mr Knotweed and Arthur said. They *can't* get sick. And if Hus can't either, what is it if it's not an illness?"

Eglantine watched as Arthur rubbed at his neck and her throat went suddenly dry.

Arthur looked from Myrtle to her, and she saw the worry in his own eyes.

"I think it's a curse."

"A curse?" gasped Eglantine. "Why do you say *that*?"

"Because there is only one thing that can affect all of us like this," said Arthur.

"What?"

"*Magic.* It's the thing that brought us to life – or back to life, as I have often said, as there are records that we may have been around before the Quake."

"Really?" asked Myrtle, looking interested.

Eglantine quickly made to interrupt one of Arthur's historical lectures. "We don't have time to get into that now," she said, exasperated.

He agreed. "Well, anyway, the only thing that could mimic an illness in us would likely be the result of a spell or a curse."

"What's the difference?" asked Myrtle.

"I think if it was just one of us, it could be a spell. But as this is affecting us all, a curse seems more likely. A curse is harder to stop."

Everyone looked horrified.

"Who would curse magical creatures and houses?" asked Eglantine.

"I don't know," said Myrtle.

Eglantine thought about her Uncle Lichen. Myrtle had said the fact that he had been promoted was fishy. Was he behind this somehow? Maybe he thought that if he couldn't get Huswyvern for himself, he'd find a way to make sure she didn't either...

But she dismissed the idea. Lichen didn't have magic. He wouldn't be able to curse anyone. This must come from someone powerful. Perhaps more than one person.

They all thought about it.

"Could the Department be behind this?" voiced Myrtle.

"Maybe," said Arthur. "They have always feared magical creatures would dominate them and take over the Isles."

Myrtle looked grim. "Maybe that's *the goal*, not just to make creatures weak but to eliminate them altogether? To turn them slowly back into stone."

12

THE SHAWL-OF-A-HUNDRED-DISGUISES

Eglantine turned white. Blood rushed in her ears. She looked at Arthur, saw his face fall, and felt her heart go with it.

Was that really what the Department wanted?

It was clear they thought of magical creatures as a threat to their power. Maybe they had decided to do something about that. Just like they ensured the "wrong" sorts of children, like girls, no longer got magic. If they allowed girls and children from poorer backgrounds to have powers, it might mean that in the future the people who run the country were not the same as the ones who always had.

Eglantine saw it now. "This must be what Miss Hegotty sensed. Binding children's magic is part of a larger picture. The Department wants to have total control over who does and doesn't have magic. They will get rid of anyone who's in their way. No matter the cost, *or the lives they take.*"

Arthur turned a pale green.

Eglantine's best friend in the entire world and her home could both turn back into lifeless stone.

"I think I might be sick," she said.

"I'm so sorry," said Myrtle.

"It's not your fault," said Arthur hotly. "We've had our heads in the sand until now, trying to cure Hus's cold, not realizing it was part of something else. It's horrible, and I won't pretend I'm not... terrified," he said, his eyes wide. "But at least we have a bit more of an idea of what the problem is. Thanks to you, Myrtle, we have the chance to fix it now."

Eglantine stared at him, and felt a sudden rush of love and determination. "You're right. There has to be a way to break this curse."

Myrtle nodded. "Yes."

"I'll check the Grimoire as soon as we get home," said Eglantine.

"It's worth asking your father too, milady," suggested Arthur. "He's currently cataloguing a very old library that might have some of the books we need. I'll write him a letter to ask if he has come across any that mention the history of magical creatures and houses, and curses. This isn't the only banned book on the subject, I'm sure," he said, indicating the book that had been prescribed to both Eglantine and Myrtle.

"That's a good idea," said Eglantine.

"I think you should take this," said Myrtle, pointing at the book. "I'll go back to my neighbour, Mr Knotweed, and his friends, and ask about their symptoms – when they started, how long it took for Mr Knotweed's foot to turn to stone, that sort of thing. I can start to build up a picture of the effects of the curse and how long things seem to take. Gargoyles are smaller than wyverns, so maybe that's why he started showing signs first? Either way it would be good to get an idea of what we're dealing with."

"That would be very helpful. Thanks, Myrtle," said Arthur.

"I think you're going to be a brilliant journalist," agreed Eglantine.

Myrtle said, "I hope so, but more than anything I hope we find out how to stop this curse."

"Me too," said Eglantine.

Before they left, they explained to Myrtle how she could get to Huswyvern via the London portal in Big Ben and made a date for her to visit once she'd gathered as much information as she could. Eglantine also went over how the protection flowers worked. They watched as Myrtle pinned hers, which was a sprig of myrtle, to her coat.

"I know things ended a bit seriously, but, well, I have enjoyed meeting you both," said Myrtle.

Eglantine smiled back. "So have we."

"Very much so," agreed Arthur.

* * *

Later that afternoon, after another lightning-carriage, which proved just as fast and uncomfortable as the first, Eglantine and Arthur returned wearily to Huswyvern.

They were determined to look through the Grimoire to find anything they could on curses that affected magical creatures and houses.

But as they made their way towards the library, their protection flowers began to glow and change before their eyes, turning from a pink rose in Eglantine's case and a red snapdragon in Arthur's into a May flower.

A lily of the valley that began to turn black.

They turned towards one another, and gasped.

Then said at the same time: "Nandi!"

All at once their flowers changed once more to show Nandi's location. It happened just as Miss Hegotty had promised them it would if any of their members were in trouble. The flower turned bone white, and now looked like a building. A building they recognized.

"It's the Isle-Spark Magical Testing Centre!" cried Arthur.

Eglantine looked at him. "I'll go and fetch my mother's shawl."

"Good thinking," he said. Not because it was cold. But because Eglantine's mother had left her a magical piece of clothing called the shawl-of-a-hundred-disguises, which allowed the user to turn into a different person, or people. She and Arthur had used it together the previous year to visit a forbidden magic market.

The testing centre wasn't far from the London portal. It was at the town hall. Their disguise, which for the moment made them look like a very old man and woman, made them blend in rather well with some of the grandparents who were waiting for their grandchildren taking their magical tests. It was busy, despite that fact it was late afternoon.

There was a family waiting area inside that smelled faintly of cabbage. It was full of hard-backed wooden chairs and it had an old musty-looking yellow carpet. They glimpsed some children standing in the hall, through the large wooden doors that were open slightly. But as Arthur and Eglantine tried to peek inside the hall, one of the instructors saw them, and said, "Sorry, the only ones allowed here are children taking their tests, and staff," and then closed the doors.

They went to take their seats in the waiting area.

"Did you see Nandi or any of the others?" whispered Arthur. He kept his voice low, even though he had put a muffle stone beneath their seats as soon as he sat down.

Eglantine shook her head. Then she began to retie the shawl, and they both changed to look like a middle-aged man with a bowler hat and a tall woman with black hair.

"What are you doing?" hissed Arthur, in horror. "What if someone saw us change right before their eyes?"

Eglantine's eyes widened. "Whoops, wasn't thinking." She looked up and scanned the area, noticing a tiny room at the back where she could spy some cups and saucers. "That must be the kitchen...it looks empty, come on," she said. He picked up the muffle stone, and they shuffled together under the shawl towards the empty kitchen.

It was a small space. Eglantine could have touched both walls with her arms, if she stretched out. There was a steel counter, topped with a large brass spark-kettle, milk, several cups and saucers, and a tin canister filled with tea bags.

Eglantine went to close the door.

"One of these hundred disguises must be some children," she said. "We need to get inside that hall."

His eyes widened in realization, and he helped her to tie and retie the shawl around them. They changed appearance countless times, from little old ladies, to two tiny gnomes, a pair of old men, a toddler and an older woman, then teenagers, a dragon and a gargoyle, children who were too young, then too old, and then finally children of about the right age, around nine years old. They looked like a pair of twin boys, with matching strawberry-blond curly hair and bright-green eyes.

They grinned at each other and were about to step outside, when the door banged open and an old woman with grey hair and half-moon glasses and a twinkly sort of smile came inside wheeling a tea trolley. "I thought I'd find you here."

Eglantine and Arthur swallowed, preparing to make up some excuse, but to their surprise, the old lady nudged the door closed, and said, "The shawl will be perfect for what we need. Thank goodness you've come. Would you mind pretending to take the test?"

For a moment, they stared at the old woman in shock that turned quickly into relief.

"Miss Hegotty?"

The older woman winked. "Nandi is safe. I've sent the others speed-mail letters, to tell them not to come. But there is something you can help us with."

The speed-mail letter explained why they hadn't seen Victoria, Eoin or Myrtle at the testing centre yet.

"What is it? Is anyone else in danger?" asked Arthur.

Miss Hegotty shook her head. "Miss Luthuli managed to intervene with some of her forget-a-lot seeds, which has altered the memory of the person who was testing Nandi's magic. It caused something of a ruckus when the instructor saw that the girl she thought she was testing turned into someone else entirely. Nandi transformed back into her real self when her magic was bound. But don't worry, she and her mother are fine. Miss Luthuli is unbinding her magic as we speak."

Arthur gasped. "So, it's true, the test binds children's magic."

Miss Hegotty nodded.

"It's the spark-staff itself. When Nandi did her test, I was hovering nearby with my trolley, and I noticed that underneath the lever they push to measure a child's magic levels, there is another hidden button. When they push that, it binds magic. All we need now to prove the Department is binding children's magic is to get our hands on one of these staffs."

They nodded.

"The Department really is evil," said Eglantine, thinking back to her own test and how excited she had been at the thought of getting magic. Her Uncle Lichen had admitted that he'd been the one to arrange having her magic bound. She couldn't help wondering if it was at a site like this. Was there a list somewhere of the children they decided to bind?

"You met with Myrtle?"

"We did," said Eglantine.

"How did it go?"

Before they could answer, Miss Hegotty's eyes turned cloudy, and she frowned as if she was struggling to see something, and then her expression cleared.

"It's all connected to the Department," breathed Miss Hegotty in wonder.

"Yes," said Eglantine, who realized that the witch must have sensed now that the "puzzle-pieces" – Myrtle and Eglantine – had connected. "When we met Myrtle, we saw what you had been sensing. That this – binding children's magic – is part of a bigger picture. The Department aren't just deciding who gets magic, but who gets to live."

There air grew heavy for a moment.

Miss Hegotty closed her eyes in horror. When she opened them, she nodded, and they continued telling her about what they had discovered – about the curse that had been placed on magical creatures and how if they didn't find a spell to stop it, magic creatures and houses would all turn back to stone.

Miss Hegotty looked bleak. "I knew it was something big, something dark, but not *that*. They are even more corrupt than I ever could have imagined. And you're right, Eglantine, evil is the word. I knew my half-brother was bad, but this is *abominable*. I will let Mrs Kusum – my departmental contact who is trying to find a way to end the corruption from within – know what we have found. Together we will find a way to stop this. We won't let them succeed," she assured them.

"But right now, we need to get a spark-staff – that's why I need your help."

Then she told them her plan.

Ten minutes later, Eglantine and Arthur followed the tea lady into the hall, and prepared to take their magic test.

Miss Hegotty's magic was powerful, and the names of two boys that hadn't been on the instructor's list a minute before, suddenly appeared without him noticing.

The instructor, a short man with dark hair combed over to one side of his head, called out for, "Archie and Ben Roberts?" and Eglantine and Arthur stepped forward. "I believe you are taking your test together?" he said, frowning at the clipboard.

"That's us," said Arthur. The instructor waved them forward. Then passed the spark-staff over them, Eglantine watched his fingers, then noticed that they were making for the button below the main lever. She quickly created a small wind to allow her to blow the forget-a-lot seeds Miss Hegotty had given them into his face.

He stared back at them with a blank look, and Arthur took the staff from him, and placed it under the shawl-of-a-hundred-disguises.

Right at that moment, Miss Hegotty's tea trolley fell over, and everyone in the hall turned to look.

"Oh, dearie me, how clumsy," the tea lady cried, and several instructors rushed forward to help.

In the kerfuffle, Eglantine and Arthur rushed out of the hall with the stolen spark-staff.

They were joined at headquarters an hour later by Miss Hegotty, Nandi and Miss Luthuli. Nandi stared at the spark-staff on the table in disgust.

"I can't believe this is how they've been binding children's magic this whole time."

The others nodded. It was shocking.

"At least now we will be able to prove that what we've been saying about the Department is right. They are corrupt."

"Yes," said Miss Hegotty.

"When are we going to go public with what we've discovered?" asked Miss Luthuli.

Miss Hegotty sighed. "Not yet. Based on what Eglantine and Arthur discovered today, the Department are more dangerous than we ever imagined. We believe they have placed a curse on magical creatures and houses."

Her words led to an uproar.

"What?" cried Miss Luthuli and Nandi.

Eglantine and Arthur filled them in on what they had found out about the mysterious illness affecting houses and creatures and how it could only be the result of a curse.

"You know for sure it's the Department?" asked Miss Luthuli.

"We don't have proof, but it makes sense that they are behind it," said Eglantine.

Miss Luthuli said, "You're right, this is much bigger than we realized. To prove this is going to be really hard."

Miss Hegotty agreed. "But before we do that, we need to find a cure. That must be our priority now."

Everyone was in agreement.

They all made plans to research how to break curses, and before they left, agreed to return within the week to share whatever they found.

Miss Hegotty turned to Eglantine and Arthur before she stepped through the portal door. "I'm sure you will fill Victoria in with all that is happening when she visits tomorrow."

And on that mysterious note, she was gone.

13

HUS IS FRUSTRATED

It had been an extremely long day, and while Eglantine felt like she should go straight to the library to begin poring over the Grimoire and other books for anything that might help them fight the curse, she was barely able to keep her eyes open. It was the same for Arthur, who suggested they turn in for the night after a light supper of sandwiches, and tackle the problem in the morning.

For once, she didn't fight him. The truth was she was no use to Hus if she couldn't think straight and she had a feeling they were going to need all the brainpower they had to solve this problem.

She couldn't lose Hus and Arthur.

Or Tidbit.

* * *

Eglantine woke up after nine in the morning. The events of the past few days had taken their toll, and at first she thought she was cold because she hadn't been feeling well. But when a snowflake fluttered onto her face, she sat up in shock.

It was snowing lightly inside. She felt Hus shiver. It must be a symptom of its illness, a result of the curse. Whatever Hus was feeling, it wasn't *good*.

Eglantine patted the wall, feeling even more determined after a full night's sleep. "We will find a way to break this curse, Hus, if it's the last thing we do."

Thankfully by the time she made her way to the library, the snow had stopped falling.

She found Arthur waiting with a plate of breakfast buns. They were both a welcome sight.

"I had a feeling you'd come here first," he said with a grin. "I'm glad to see you looking more rested."

Eglantine was more interested in how he was feeling. He was the one affected by the curse. "And you – how do you feel?" she asked worriedly, her eyes trailing over him.

"Not bad, honestly. Better for the early night."

She was glad to hear that.

"Before we start looking through the Grimoire and library for counter-curses, I'll write to your father."

"Good idea," she said, helping herself to a breakfast bun.

The library in Wales that had donated its books to the Isle-Spark Museum contained some of the oldest books since the discovery of isle-spark magic, so it was possible her father would find something on magical creatures and houses while he was sorting through the books.

"Just don't tell him why you're asking. He'll only panic and come home and, to be honest, he'd be more useful there, looking for any books that might help."

"You're right," said Arthur. "I don't like keeping something like this from him, though, it feels rather big, and technically, I'm staff, so…"

Eglantine frowned at him. "You're family, Arthur. But I see your point. Let me write the letter instead, say it's something I need for my schoolwork. It's probably easier for me to fib than you…"

"Thank you," said Arthur, who found lying almost impossible.

It took several attempts but eventually she had written a letter to her father that she hoped wouldn't cause him to worry.

Dear Father,

I hope you are well and that you are enjoying your time in Wales. I'm writing to ask for your assistance with academic research for an examination I am taking soon. It concerns the history of magical creatures and any curses they may or may not have endured in the past and how they were broken. I was told that this information would likely only be available in very old books, like the ones you are sorting through now, so if you could send me excerpts of anything useful, I would be most grateful.

With love,
Eglantine

PS We are fine. Arthur sends "great affection" and The Boots have taken to sleeping in your room, so I think they are missing you too.

PPS Tidbit made your favourite biscuits, I hope you enjoy them.

PPPS She only threw one pan at me when I made the request, so I think that means she misses you too.

Once she'd finished the letter, she fetched the Grimoire. "I want to be methodical and go over every spell that mentions a curse and how to break it."

Just as she was about to take a firm hold of the book, snow began to fall again, thick and heavy inside the house, covering everything in a blanket of white. This was far worse than the snow she had woken up to that morning. The temperature fell to below freezing. Clearly Hus was feeling worse. After wading through waist-high drifts in the library, Eglantine used her magic to create watercolour vines that she cast onto the banisters so that she could swing herself down the stairs.

To her horror, winter had taken over everywhere else in the house too. The grand staircase was covered in snow. The spark-chandeliers above flickered then died, and she came across Arthur, who was flying towards her carrying blankets and scarves.

"Thanks," she said, reaching for a blanket.

"I think we might actually be warmer outside for once," he said, leading her cold and shivering to the gardens.

It felt wrong to leave Hus when it was clearly feeling miserable and out of control, but as the temperature inside right then was closer to what it might have been in Antarctica, it was the only option. Arthur broke off some of the vines that had frozen around her little arm, and then set about making a fire in a barrel in the garden. Eglantine turned to look at the falling snow inside the house, which was still coming in thick drifts.

"Oh, poor Hus, this is awful."

There was a sound like a sniffle from the walls.

The house let out a great big, weary sigh.

It took hours for the snow to melt, and then they were left with the mess.

As day turned to night, Eglantine got to work, performing some of the fire spells she had learned during her first year of Miss Hegotty's course. Arthur flew around, drying curtains with the steam from his nostrils.

The library was in high dudgeon. All the books were sulking and taking turns to dry themselves off by a crackling fire that Hus had started itself.

The coat rack and The Boots were rushing around, trying their best to make things right, but there was a sense of weariness in everyone.

One of the only things that made it slightly better was the arrival of Victoria, who came through her portal door and immediately pitched in to help.

"I'm so glad you're here," said Eglantine, and she told her everything that had happened since she saw her last, from the magical testing centre to the discovery of the curse.

Victoria was shocked.

"That's despicable – they've cursed them to slowly turn back into stone?"

Then she blinked, and gasped, her hand covering her mouth.

"Conroy," she said.

"Conroy?" repeated Arthur.

They knew she was referring to the comptroller at the palace, but not why.

"The secret meetings he's been having with Lord Ragwort. Twice now I've overheard them say that the plan is in alignment, but the last time I heard Ragwort say, 'Finally, those cursed beasts will get what they deserve.' I assumed he meant people he didn't like in government, not magical creatures, because Ragwort often refers to people he doesn't like as 'beasts' – but maybe he meant magical creatures?"

Eglantine and Arthur gaped at her.

"So, the Department *really* is behind this curse," said Arthur in horror.

"Yes. The only thing is, we've got to find a way to prove it," said Victoria.

"Before we do anything, we need to try and break the curse," reminded Eglantine.

"You're right," said Victoria.

Eglantine went to the Grimoire again.

But, to her frustration, the book flipped quickly past the beginning towards the spell scrap at the back.

Her first instinct was to grab hold of the book like she normally did, but this time she frowned and lifted her hand away from the book.

Something about this spell scrap. There were just a few words remaining, none of which appeared to make any sense.

"It has been doing this since it first got ill," said Eglantine. "What are you trying to tell me?" she asked Hus. "Will this spell help us to break the curse?"

Victoria and Arthur sat up straight.

The chairs nodded but the books shook themselves.

"I'm confused."

There was a sigh from the fireplace.

"Is there a way to restore this spell?" asked Victoria.

The footstool shook itself.

Arthur frowned. "Maybe we can find this spell somewhere else, is that what you're saying?"

The books once again shook themselves.

The furniture slumped and there was a sigh from deep within the bowels of the house.

Eglantine glanced around and frowned.

She couldn't help feeling frustrated, and she knew that Hus was feeling that too.

"I don't know what you're trying to tell us, Hus," she said.

Then, to her dismay, she felt something that really would only make matters worse.

She was tired and stressed and she closed her eyes in disbelief.

Hus was about to sneeze, *again*.

After the long evening they had had clearing up the mess from the snowstorm earlier, she couldn't help the sudden flash of annoyance, mixed with worry. It was getting worse.

"Hus is about to blow."

"Oh, no," said Victoria with a heavy sigh.

Then there was another bone-weary sigh from the house. A sigh that turned into something *else.*

Hus sucked in a breath and a howling wind whipped across the room, lifting both girls off their feet and flinging them through the just-opened London portal door, taking their panicked screams with them.

"No!" cried Arthur, rushing after them.

But by the time he got to the door, it was too late.

They were *gone.*

14

BACK IN TIME

The portal began to spin.

When at last it came to a halt, Eglantine and Victoria stumbled out and fell into a pile of leaves. Victoria was sick at the foot of Big Ben.

Eglantine looked up wearily to see a sky blanketed by night and fog. Soon one heavy clang of its bell followed after another, and rattled the teeth inside her head, as the clock began to chime midnight.

Outside there was the *clip-clop* of hooves as a carriage went past.

She made her way on jelly legs to help Victoria to stand. The princess wiped her mouth and swayed on her feet.

Reflected back in her eyes was the sweeping vista of the Palace of Westminster. She looked at it in confusion.

"W-what just happened?"

Eglantine stared back at the door. "We were flung through the London portal."

Victoria looked confused, as she took in the sights around her. There was a faint breeze, and the scent of the river was briny and yet not unpleasant.

"Do you think Hus meant to do that?"

"It felt deliberate."

"But why? Because it was frustrated?"

Eglantine shook her head. "No, this is something else. I'm sure of it."

They stepped back inside Hus.

Instinctively, Eglantine reached out in her mind for her home. But there was no response.

Oh, no, she thought.

Her heart began to pound inside her ears.

"Um, Eglantine, something seems…I don't know…wrong," whispered Victoria.

An old grandfather clock, its face painted with stars and moons, let out a single chime.

Like it had the last time.

The tiny scar on her forehead itched. She touched it absently.

Her throat turned dry.

Not again.

A large spider with a red dot on its body scuttled along the floor.

Eglantine stared at in shock. That had happened last time she was here too.

"What's going on – did Hus redecorate while we were gone?" asked Victoria.

"No," said Eglantine, finding her voice. "It's worse than that. It's done it again."

"Done what?"

"*Taken us back in time.*"

Victoria gasped, and looked around in a mix of wonder and fear. "Really?"

Eglantine nodded.

"This happened last time – the clock was here, and it chimed as soon as I arrived. Hus banished it years ago because it fell on me, and I'm pretty sure that was the same spider I saw," she whispered, pointing to the little creature that scuttled away.

There was a sound from around the corner. Like an intake of breath. The kind someone might make if they were afraid of being caught doing something they shouldn't...

Eglantine had a feeling that she knew what, or more specifically, *who* she was going to find.

A blond, skinny boy, wearing an old-fashioned ruffled shirt with an ink stain on the left sleeve, was hunched in the padded window seat, partially hidden behind one of the heavy red curtains. From where he was sitting, the window offered a bright and sunny view of the cliffs and the rolling sea below.

She stepped forward and the floorboards creaked.

Just as it had last time, she realized.

But this time he was the one who noticed her first. He'd heard them before the floorboard squeaked, and was already hiding something behind his back.

"Who let you in?" he demanded.

Eglantine peered around him to see what he was hiding. But he twisted away.

"Is that *Lichen*?' cried Victoria.

The boy glared at them both.

"Who's asking? Who are *you*? What are you doing here?" he demanded, his pale face outraged. "Who said you could enter this house?"

Then his nose wrinkled in apparent disgust as he stared at Eglantine. "What happened to your arm?"

Eglantine's eyes narrowed. "What happened to your face?"

Victoria snorted. The expression he was wearing, as if there was a nasty smell beneath his nose, turned his otherwise handsome face ugly.

His eyes widened in shock, his mouth fell open and he gasped. "What did you say?"

"You heard me," spat Eglantine.

Clearly, he wasn't used to anyone giving him back what he dished out.

He was still trying to hide the book he was holding away, and something about that made Eglantine leap forward to try and prise it from him, knowing that whatever he was up to, it likely wasn't good.

"Stop that!" he cried. "It's mine."

She blinked as her hand passed though the book as if it was made of air.

She'd forgotten that last time she'd come back she'd been as insubstantial as a ghost then too.

Victoria raised her hand, the way she did whenever she was using her magic. "My powers aren't working. I tried to rewind time, but nothing happened."

"You – *what?*" cried Lichen.

They ignored him. "Maybe it can't work because we're not technically alive yet?"

Victoria frowned. "Maybe."

Lichen looked very confused. "What are you both talking about?"

Eglantine stared at him, and that was when she saw it. His hand moved, and she got a glimpse of the book he was holding awkwardly, with one hand inside it, like a very uncomfortable bookmark.

Like he was afraid it would *close* if he didn't.

If she hadn't seen the title, that very action would have told her all she needed to know.

He had the Huswyvern Grimoire!

"How did you open that?" she cried in horror. Only those with magic could.

"What's it to you?" he spat. "It's mine, or at least it *would* be, if the world hadn't lost its mind!"

"What are you talking about?" said Victoria.

Eglantine answered before he could. "He means before the

law changed so that houses like Huswyvern didn't pass to the firstborn male child, but the firstborn, regardless of their gender."

Lichen looked at Eglantine in surprise. "Yes, that's exactly what I meant."

"Why, you selfish little—" snapped Victoria.

Lichen's eyes grew wide and he shouted. "How dare you speak to me like that! What are you even doing here? Are you ghosts? Helli is too soft, I've told her she needs to banish the lot of you!"

Eglantine stared back at him wordlessly. He'd said that to her last time too. And just like last time, soon enough there was the sound of hastening footsteps and she saw her mother.

"Can we help you?" asked Heliotrope, gazing at Eglantine and Victoria, a bemused look on her face. Only to gasp in sudden horror as she looked from Lichen to them, and noticed he was holding the spellbook.

She looked at them all in suspicion, drawing her own conclusions. "Did you help him to open it? Is he trying to sell you this?!"

Now Eglantine understood why she had been so upset last time. Her mother had thought that she was there to take the spellbook!

"We didn't help him to open it, we wouldn't!" cried Victoria.

"We're trying to figure out why he has it at all," agreed Eglantine.

"*You're* the one who left it open, sister," said Lichen. "So I decided to have a look, and that's when I found something very interesting... Something that would help make sure I could open this book whenever I want from now on, considering it should have been mine."

"What?" Helli made to snatch the book out of Lichen's hands, but as she did so, whatever she saw on the page that he had been so immersed in reading made her pale. "Lichen," she breathed, her eyes turning wide. "That's a forbidden curse. It's evil. I know you want magic for yourself, but not like that! If you were found using it, you could get sent to prison!"

"Only if I'm caught!"

Eglantine felt her body turn cold.

It couldn't be him...could it?

Is Lichen the one responsible for the curse? Is that why I'm here?

In her shock, she watched as Helli's hand dived for the page, while Lichen held on for dear life.

Eglantine tried to see what was on the page that had caused her mother to react so violently. As Lichen and Helli grappled with the book, Eglantine glimpsed part of the title which said: *Drawing Magic from S—* but couldn't see the rest of the word. She tried to twist around the fighting siblings for a better view, but before she could there was the sound of a page being ripped from the Grimoire, followed by Helli's triumphant yell as she held onto it.

Then Eglantine's world was spinning once more, and the next thing she knew they were outside the London portal door again, at the foot of Big Ben.

"Oh, gosh, that was horrible," breathed Victoria. "And what was that all about with young Lichen and your mother?"

When the world stopped spinning, they dared to reopen the portal door.

Eglantine staggered against the wall in relief as she felt the familiar sensation of Hus beneath her touch.

"Oh, my goodness, FINALLY!" cried Arthur, who was a very pale sort of green. "I have been out of my mind with worry!"

They were back.

15

A Time Loop

The first thing they had to do was calm Arthur down.

The wyvern-butler was, understandably, in something of a state, having witnessed an indoor twister whisk Eglantine and Victoria off the ground, and hurtle them through a portal door.

"You've been gone for an hour!"

"Have we?' said Victoria, who looked more curious than concerned. "How interesting!"

"INTERESTING! I feel like I have aged another hundred years," Arthur said.

"Sorry, Arthur," said Eglantine, though it was hardly her fault that Hus had taken them back in time.

The coat rack patted Arthur on the back in sympathy.

"Okay, tell me again. What happened? I'm calm now. You went back in time again, yes?"

"Yes," said Eglantine as Victoria shook her head and said, "Well, sort of."

They both turned to look at Victoria in surprise.

"What do you mean, sort of?" said Eglantine hotly, her brow furrowing in confusion. "You were *there*, you saw what happened!"

"Yes, I'm not denying that," she said, holding up a hand as if to pacify Eglantine, who had opened her mouth to argue that she seemed to be doing *exactly that*. "What I'm saying is perhaps we travelled to a time loop."

They both frowned.

"A time *loop*?" asked Eglantine.

"Yes," said Victoria, explaining further. "It's a moment in time that is preserved, that can reset itself again. I suspect that once we left, it reset itself to how it always goes. You said it yourself that you had been to that exact moment before."

Eglantine thought about the spider, the chime of the grandfather clock, and Lichen hidden away in the exact same spot. It *had* been the same as before.

"I think Hus created it in order to show you a memory it wanted you to see. The loop means that we can't really change things. Once we left, your uncle and mother would have no memory that we were ever there."

Eglantine frowned. Victoria was right. "Hus wanted to show me that moment. It took us there *on purpose*," she breathed.

The feeling she'd had earlier as she heard her mother call the curse Lichen had been reading "evil" washed over her again.

"It *is* Lichen," she said. "He's the one behind the curse."

Arthur and Victoria gasped.

Eglantine's eyes widened as she remembered what her mother's ghost had said about it trying to her show her something. She must have meant Hus. "Hus has been trying to show us all along. Lichen stole a spell out of the Grimoire. A *forbidden curse* – that's what my mother said."

The coat rack nodded, then appeared to sag, relieved that, at last, it had got its message through.

Eglantine felt tears prick her eyes, and a rush of love for her house as she touched the table in apology. "I'm sorry I didn't work it out sooner, Hus."

The armchair reached out to pat her hand.

The Grimoire opened of its own accord to the back page.

They all looked at it.

Victoria rushed over. "This must have been the curse Lichen was looking at. The one your mother said he would go to prison for if he used it."

Arthur looked confused, scratching a talon along his chin.

"But he doesn't have magic. It's not like he could have cast a curse without it."

Eglantine stared at him, then frowned. "The last thing my mother said to him before we left was: 'I know you want magic for yourself but not like that!' She called it *evil.* It was hard to see what the spell was called. But I think it was titled *Drawing Magic from S—*"

Arthur exhaled sharply. "From stone?" he guessed. "This must be it. The curse."

They stared at each other in horror.

"But why would he have waited so long to do it? I mean, if Lichen stole it, it was years ago. But the last time we saw him, he didn't have magic," said Arthur. "Otherwise he would have used it on you."

Victoria frowned. "I don't think he got the spell back then. In the time loop, before we left, Eglantine's mother managed to tear the curse out of the book."

"Yes," agreed Eglantine. She had seen the same thing.

She closed her eyes for a beat as she realized...

"*That's what my mother meant.*"

They stared at her in confusion.

"My mother's ghost told me that Hus was trying to show me something and I needed to listen. Right? But before she left, she said, 'It's all my fault. I should have destroyed it, not hidden it where it could be found.' That means somehow Lichen found the curse she had ripped out."

Arthur gasped. "It fits – last year when he broke into the eastern wing! Maybe he found it there, amongst her things!"

Eglantine gaped at him in horror.

He was right. The eastern wing had been where Hus's magic had faded last year, but it had also once been her mother's childhood bedroom, where she had hidden the Grimoire before she died. She had come back to show Eglantine the hiding place in her ghostly form. It wasn't hard to believe she had hidden the forbidden curse there too.

"Is that what you've been trying to tell us, Hus?" she asked. "That Lichen found it?"

Everything about Hus was nodding.

It had been trying to tell her this whole time.

"Alright, Hus. What else have we missed?"

Suddenly, the Grimoire closed then flipped furiously as it had so often to the last page. To where the tiny spell scrap remained.

It was a small, jagged bit of paper at the bottom of the page, only a few centimetres across. With just a few scattered words.

Eglantine switched on one of the spark-lamps and put the book underneath to read the jumble of words that remained.

They stared at it.

"*Counter?*" said Victoria with a frown. She stared at the spell scrap. There was a faint mark next to the word *counter*, like a bit of dirt. She scratched at it with a fingernail and they gasped as behind the fleck of dirt was a word, or part of one that had been torn away. Now the snippet read:

"As in a counter-*curse*?" breathed Eglantine.

16

THE EMERGENCY MEETING

It was raining in London. The streets were covered in fallen autumn leaves that crunched underfoot. Big Ben chimed the noon hour. Crowds of people dressed in shades of black, beige and grey rushed past the cobbled streets alongside spark-carriages that trundled on, horseless, past the River Thames.

A spark-powered narrowboat carrying a load of enchanted music boxes drifted past, the captain humming a tune along with one of the devices.

Myrtle shivered in her coat and brushed down the fabric of her good navy skirt. She stood before the portal door that no one else seemed able to see, right at the foot of the great clock.

It glowed with a strange blue light. She watched as people walked quickly by, and wondered what they saw instead.

Her protection flower had changed into the shape of a multicoloured gothic house, which she knew was the signal that a society meeting had been called.

She was here at last.

It had been two days since she joined, and had met Eglantine and Arthur at the cafe.

Since then she'd met up with her neighbour Mr Knotweed and his friends to figure out a timeline for how long it seemed to take before they began to turn into stone.

She took a deep breath. She was not looking forward to sharing the bad news.

But, she reminded herself, it wasn't likely that an emergency meeting had been called for good news, so she would be in good company.

"Don't be nervous," she told herself.

Someone forgot to tell her knees, which shook like a blizzard.

Suddenly a knocker appeared, and before she could lift a hand to it, the door opened, and Eglantine whipped her blond head left and right before pulling Myrtle, lightning fast, by the hand through the portal.

The door closed behind her and Myrtle jumped.

"Sorry about that, thought I'd get you inside in case the portal did anything mad. It's been glitching as a result of its cold – er – *curse*," she said, wincing.

"Oh, the poor thing," said Myrtle.

"So, you found us alright? How was the lighting-carriage?"

"Yes, fine. It was brilliant. I got here in less than twenty minutes."

Eglantine nodded. "It's amazing how they are the longest twenty minutes of your life, though, right?"

Myrtle snickered. "I didn't mind it too much, but I can see how it wouldn't be everyone's cup of tea."

Eglantine grinned. "Well, anyway, welcome. Everyone else is here."

"Thanks," said Myrtle, turning with wide eyes to take in her surroundings. This wasn't London any more. She was in some kind of a handsome study. There was a large table, at which several people were already sitting and waiting. Next to it was a fireplace, topped by a figure of the one-armed battle hero Sorcerer Nelson, who doffed his tricorn at her. The window on the opposite wall showed a view of the sea.

Arthur rushed forward. "Greetings, Myrtle, welcome to headquarters." He introduced her to the others. A boy with a rat on his shoulder, named Eoin, and an attractive older woman and her daughter, Miss Luthuli and Nandi. And then, wait, was that— No. Her eyes widened into saucers.

It was.

"Your Royal Highness," she said, sinking into a rather awkward curtsy that started off as a kind of bow before she remembered.

"Please, call me Victoria," said the princess.

"Blimey," said Myrtle, blushing furiously. "I mean—"

"No, that about sums it up perfectly," said the boy, and they all laughed.

Behind the princess was another figure. She was tall, with

dark-blond hair, and sharply intelligent eyes. "It is a pleasure to meet you in person at last," said Miss Hegotty. "Welcome to your first meeting. I can only apologize that it is an emergency one, and so thank you for coming, especially from so far."

"It is a pleasure to meet you too," said Myrtle, feeling a bit awed as she took a seat. "It was no trouble."

Miss Hegotty smiled. "We called the meeting because we have discovered the person behind the curse."

There were gasps from Eoin, Nandi and Miss Luthuli.

"Who?" cried Nandi.

"It was Lichen."

Eoin's mouth gaped. Then his face turned blotchy in anger. "Lichen!"

"Your uncle?" said Myrtle to Eglantine.

Eglantine inclined her head. "He is also, unfortunately, Eoin's father," she said, shooting the boy a sympathetic look.

"We found out it was him last night," said Eglantine, and filled them in on how the house had taken her and Victoria back in time, and how it had been trying to tell her all along that her uncle had stolen a forbidden curse that leached magic from stone creatures and houses.

"The stolen magic will go to Lichen."

They gasped in horror at that.

"I can't believe that this whole time it was him," said Miss Luthuli in horror.

"Me neither, or that he's found another way to take Huswyvern from you!" cried Nandi.

"I can," spat Eoin. "He might be my father, but I have never known anyone as callous as him."

Eglantine, who had deep circles under her eyes, nodded. "This is worse than last year, though. This...this is evil. To take magic from creatures? He knows Arthur. He claims to love Hus, and yet he would do this?"

"You're right. His motive seems altogether more sinister," agreed Miss Hegotty. "I believe what we are facing here is called a creeping curse, because it creeps slowly over time. It's one of the worst forms of curses, because it's so hard to detect at first, and by the time most realize, it's too late."

The room grew quiet.

"How do we know for sure that that is the kind of curse he used?" asked Eoin.

It was Myrtle who answered. "I think it must be. The past few days, I've been to visit my neighbour Mr Knotweed's friends. All their symptoms started the same way – first with flu-like symptoms, then a rash, and eventually parts of them began to turn to stone. That took about a month. The smaller creatures developed symptoms earlier, and the larger creatures have only recently started showing symptoms, but they all seem to follow the same path."

Everyone stared at her. "So, after a month I could start turning to stone?" breathed Arthur.

They all exclaimed in horror.

"It could be shorter."

The silence was horribly loud after that.

Eoin snapped angrily. "Why? Why would he do this?! The more I know about him the more I *despise* him. There are much easier ways to get magic! Did he just not know another way?"

"I doubt it," said Eglantine. "I mean he was responsible for binding my magic, so he must know the reverse is possible."

Miss Hegotty's lips thinned. "Yes. But from what we know of Lichen, he's ruthless and scheming. He wouldn't choose a path like my course – it would have meant he had to work at it, the way all of you had to. It's simple to unlock your magic, but it's not without effort. He's taken an easy way—"

"EASY?" cried Eoin in horror. "Stealing magic from creatures and homes and turning them to stone – that's easy?"

"If you don't have a conscience, yes," said Eglantine.

Miss Hegotty nodded. "He would be willing to do that if it meant he could get powers almost instantly, and soon he will be very powerful indeed."

"What is he going to do with all that power?" breathed Nandi.

They shared worried looks.

Myrtle frowned. "Maybe it's not *just* about the power for him. We're assuming that's his ultimate goal, but, well, as you say, he could have got magic before, so maybe it's about what this curse will eventually do that interests him…"

Eglantine wasn't the only one to gasp in sudden realization.

"The curse will eventually turn all the magic creatures to stone!" breathed Arthur. "Perhaps he used this curse so that he could get ahead – and perhaps even clear his name. Maybe it's *why* he was promoted to the head of the Banned Magic Office."

"I don't follow," said Nandi. "Why would the curse help him to get ahead or clear his name?"

Arthur explained. "The Department has never made it a secret that it sees magical creatures as a problem. Perhaps Lichen told them he had a way to get rid of us for ever."

Myrtle's eyes widened. She looked grim. "That's what the news has really been about – a kind of propaganda campaign. It's what we were speaking about when we met – in recent months' people have begun to fear magical creatures, thanks to all those articles in the papers. Maybe they've done that so that when magical creatures turn to stone, instead of asking questions, people are... relieved?"

It was a truly horrible thought.

"This is appalling. We have to stop them," said Victoria. "Perhaps we could go and see the king? We can't let them get away with this!"

Everyone voiced their agreement.

Miss Hegotty looked determined. "They will *not* get away with this. We will make them face these crimes. If it's the last thing I do."

She looked so fierce and angry that everyone started to speak at once, to state that they would do the same.

Miss Hegotty nodded. "Good. But right now, we don't have any proof. Myrtle and the others have done excellent work in finding out what they can, and from the evidence Myrtle has gathered, it's clear we don't have the luxury of time. We have to focus on finding the counter-curse, and then we will make it our mission to prove what they have done. I promise you that."

Miss Hegotty was right. This had to be the priority. Huswyvern, Arthur and all their magical friends' lives depended on them finding a way to break the curse.

"Can I see the remainder of the spell in the Grimoire?" asked Miss Hegotty.

Eglantine brought the spellbook to her, which opened by itself to the last page, where just the small scrap of jagged paper remained.

Miss Hegotty reached inside her coat for a monocle on a chain, which she lifted to her eye to read the remainder better.

"Perhaps it might respond to a restoration incantation," she mused. She raised her hands, and they saw a cascade of shimmery purple light emerge from her fingertips, while she spoke an incantation over the page.

Eglantine held her breath. If they could read the spell, perhaps they could reverse it.

Nothing happened.

"Hmmm," Miss Hegotty said with a sigh. She frowned, patted down her coat pockets and then fished out a stub of a black candle. "Perhaps it will reveal itself with this," she said.

"Of course," said Eglantine. "A revelation candle."

Miss Hegotty lit the candle, and performed a spell.

By the light of this flame
Let the smoke reveal
The spell that once remained

The revelation candle produced a bright blue smoke that flickered in the air, then turned completely black, before a gust of wind arrived and the smoke vanished without a trace.

Miss Hegotty raised a brow.

"We cannot restore it. It was designed to be only written down once."

They all shared looks of concern.

"So, what does that mean for us?" said Victoria.

"It means we need to find out the rest of what was written here," she said, looking at the spell scrap.

Eoin got up to peer at the words, along with the others. "Maybe we can guess some of it?"

Eglantine agreed. "We guessed already that *Counter-cur*— likely means a counter-curse, but I'm not sure what stars or 'the Witchlight' could mean. Does anyone else have any ideas?"

Everyone shook their heads.

Almost everyone.

Myrtle gasped in recognition. "I-I don't know what it is or what it means, but I have heard those words, many times."

They all stared at her.

"What? From where?" asked Eglantine.

"My father's ghost," she breathed. "It's the thing he keeps trying to warn me about."

17

THE LAST MEMORY

Myrtle's pronouncement caused pandemonium.

They all stared at her in shock as she explained further.

"My father died when his pub burned down six months ago. Ever since he first appeared in ghost form, he's been saying, 'The fires are connected. I have to tell them about the Witchlight. Before the planets align.' The Department came to investigate, but concluded there wasn't a connection to the fire in the palace at Westminster, which is what I assumed he meant, as that fire happened at a similar time. But the Department said the fire in our pub was the result of a faulty oven."

Eglantine realized in shock that she had read about Myrtle's story in the papers only recently.

Eoin looked at Myrtle with a raised brow. "The same

Department who bind children's magic, curse magical creatures and houses. That Department? It's not possible that they've just *lied*?"

Myrtle closed her eyes in horror. "Oh, God, you're right. Of course you're right. They *lied*," she whispered.

Eglantine shot Eoin a remonstrative look, and he winced. Even Rat Lord Byron smacked a claw at him for his lack of tact.

"How did I not see that?" whispered Myrtle.

Eglantine comforted her. "They're good at their lies. That's how they've managed to do what they've done for so long."

"That's a good point. I just wish I had unlocked my truth-detecting Witchspark sooner..." Myrtle looked at Eglantine. "You said when we met that there was a spell I could use to try to communicate with my father's ghost?"

Eglantine agreed. "There is. I've seen it in the Grimoire. But..." She hesitated.

"What?"

"It's, well...it will be hard."

"I don't mind a complicated spell."

"No, it's not that. I don't think it's overly complex. I mean that it will be hard, *emotionally*."

She fetched the Grimoire, and as if the book knew exactly what spell Eglantine was referring to it opened onto a page entitled: *Ghost Memory Spell*.

Miss Hegotty looked a bit concerned as Myrtle read the words. "I see what you mean. This should work. You said you've found it hard to speak to him. I think that might be because he is trapped, in a sense. With ghosts, they can sometimes get locked inside a memory. Their last memory. With this spell, he'll be able to show it to you."

Myrtle drew in a shaky breath.

Eglantine looked uneasy. "To see one of your parents die – that could haunt you for ever."

Everyone started speaking at once.

"Myrtle doesn't need to see it – but one of us should. We can't ignore this, it might help us to break the curse," said Eoin.

Myrtle shook her head. "I want to know what happened to him."

They all stared at her.

She continued in a rush. "You don't understand. I've wondered about this for so long. Wondered why he haunts his business but not me, why that seemed more important than his only child. If… if it wasn't an accident…if he's come back to warn us about something connected with Lichen and this curse, I *need* to know."

Miss Hegotty placed a hand on Myrtle's shoulder.

"I think it's best then, if Myrtle, Arthur and Eglantine go tonight to Edinburgh to visit his ghost and cast the spell to witness his last memory," said Miss Hegotty. "Victoria will likely need to get back soon, before they notice your absence at the palace."

Victoria sighed. "Yes." She glanced at Eoin. "We should go."

Eoin hesitated. "No one notices if I'm not around. It's not like the carriages get taken out often enough. I'm usually just doing odd jobs to fill the time. I can easily slip in and out of the palace, and back again. I think it would make sense if we begin tracking Lichen, seeing what he's up to, who he's meeting and that sort of thing."

Miss Hegotty hesitated. "It could be dangerous."

"I'll be careful. Besides, I can't stop thinking about why this curse would be in the Grimoire in the first place, because there's no way the book would want anyone to cast this awful spell. I'm guessing you need to understand how the curse works before you can perform the counter-curse, so if Lichen has the curse…he might have the reverse too."

Eglantine's eyes widened in realization. "You think he's keeping that safe somewhere?"

Eoin nodded. "Yes."

"Track him, but don't try and find it yourself. If he's keeping it safe, we don't want him to get rid of it in a panic," said Miss Hegotty.

"Alright."

"Just take care," said Arthur.

"Let us know if you need our help," said Miss Luthuli. "Now that we have finished our undercover mission at the testing centre, we are free to be of service."

"Thanks. Probably less conspicuous if it's just me for now."

Myrtle looked puzzled. "Undercover mission?" she asked.

Eglantine said, "I will fill you in later." Then she looked at Eoin. "Speaking of being less conspicuous: use my mother's shawl," she said, rushing to fetch it for him.

* * *

An hour later, Eglantine found herself whizzing through the countryside on her way to Edinburgh and feeling decidedly sick as she sat across from Arthur and Myrtle in the lightning-carriage.

When they came to a jolting stop, a brass counter displayed the number eighteen on a panel to the left, and a disembodied female voice said, "Good news. We have arrived at your destination earlier than expected. Remember to tip your driver." A slot appeared above the door handle. Eglantine wearily dropped in a sixpence, fighting the urge to bring up her dinner.

They climbed down from the carriage and out into a cold, wet night, lit up by spark-street-lamps.

"It's there," said Myrtle softly, pointing.

They were standing around the corner from a charred building.

Myrtle took a breath, and began to walk towards it. Eglantine and Arthur followed.

As they rounded the corner, they saw the ghost of Myrtle's father, George Chan, waiting on the street opposite his old pub.

A sign above the door was blackened in places, but they could make out that it read: *The Witch's Cat.*

"Hello, Father," said Myrtle, going to stand next to him. Eglantine and Arthur stood a little behind.

He didn't acknowledge them, just stared woodenly at his old pub.

After a while he muttered, "I have to warn them."

Myrtle said, "I know."

He turned to look at her, and, from the surprise on her face, they could see he didn't usually. Myrtle blinked at him in shock. "Father, can you see me? Do you recognize me?"

He frowned, then turned his face back to the pub once more. "The fires are connected. I have to tell them about the Witchlight. Before the planets align."

"That's why we're here, Mr Chan," said Eglantine. "We want you to tell us about the fires and the Witchlight." She opened the Grimoire to the spell, and took out what looked like an odd piece of shimmery chalk from one of her coat pockets. "Memory chalk," she told the others. She bent down and drew a circle around them all, including Mr Chan. Then she told Myrtle to do the same thing but in an anticlockwise direction. When she stood up, a strange light began to glow all around them.

"Ready?" asked Eglantine. Myrtle nodded, and together they recited the spell.

Spirit to earth, earth to spirit
Join together in this neutral plane
Reveal the last memory before Mr Chan departed
Show us what he saw once again

There was a sudden flash of the strange shimmery light. So bright, it was almost blinding. Eglantine held up a hand to her eyes, and then the light was gone.

She blinked as her eyes adjusted. Only to cry out in shock.

They were inside an old, cosy pub. There were several round tables and a pair of tartan armchairs faced a crackling fire in the hearth, where above it a black cauldron simmered, letting off a pleasant scent. In the smoke, every so often, a cat appeared and winked.

On the stone walls, there were paintings of cats atop flying broomsticks.

It was charming, thought Eglantine.

Beside her, she heard Myrtle swallow.

"It's the pub, before...before it burned down. He...he always loved cats."

Eglantine didn't know what to say. She reached for Myrtle's hand and squeezed.

Arthur placed a talon of support on her shoulder. "We must be inside his memory."

Night had fallen and, inside the pub, there was only one table occupied, right at the back, in a booth that was partially obscured by a half-timbered wall. From where they stood, they could see the backs of two customers. From a swinging door to their left, George Chan appeared. He looked so different from his ghostly version. Far less serious.

There was a twinkle in his brown eyes and he walked with a light step.

He had a smile on his face, revealing a dimple in one of his cheeks as he approached the customers. "Everything alright with the food? Can I get you anything else?"

A voice snapped, "Some privacy would be nice."

"Don't mind him," said a rich, cultured voice. "He's been in a mood all day."

"You would be too, if you had just found yourself *dismissed from your post.*"

Eglantine felt the hairs on her neck stand on end.

She knew that voice.

"It's Lichen!"

Arthur motioned them closer. "We're in a memory, they can't see us," he reminded them.

Eglantine and Myrtle moved to the other side of the table, and they both gasped.

"Is that Lord Ragwort?" breathed Myrtle.

"I think so," said Eglantine, whose attention was captured by her uncle.

"Only temporarily," continued Ragwort in soothing tones.

George Chan excused himself. "I shall leave you to enjoy the rest of your meal. Call me if you need anything."

Lichen waved a hand dismissively, not even glancing in Mr Chan's direction as he turned to leave.

"We need to keep up appearances, while it all gets pinned on the Whistlewitch and you're under investigation," said Ragwort.

"Keep it down, he might hear!"

"Don't worry so much."

But it turned out that Lichen had cause to worry, because George Chan had stopped in his tracks when he heard Ragwort mention the Whistlewitch. He went to stand out of sight, near a potted palm around the corner, but still in hearing distance.

"Oh, Father," whispered Myrtle, seeing him linger.

But, like Mr Chan, they too were sucked into the drama unfolding at the table.

Myrtle took something out of her pocket that looked a bit like an embroidery hoop, and she held onto it.

Eglantine was curious but she didn't say anything. She didn't want to pry. She looked back at the table as Lichen's voice rose.

"I don't see why you want to wait. We have what we need already," he spat, tapping a piece of paper on the table.

Eglantine tried to look, but couldn't see past Lichen's hand.

"The fire at the Palace of Westminster took care of any link you and I had to the Whistlewitch and our plans to steal Huswyvern, so there's no paper trail of our connection to that unfortunate bit of business. There's just that document she tried to get Lord Bury to sign against his will. So she will take the fall. All I'm asking is that you be patient for a few more months, my dear fellow," said Lord Ragwort.

Eglantine and Arthur gasped. They were admitting to it – they'd started the fire at the Palace of Westminster!

Lichen moved his hand slightly, and Myrtle's hand grabbed Eglantine's arm. "Is that..." she said, pointing at the piece of paper. "Is that the curse!?'

Eglantine gasped. "It could be!"

"Why wait, then?" said Lichen. "Thanks to this curse, I will be able to steal magic from magical creatures and homes, and when they turn back into stone, I'll have helped the Department eliminate a problem that has been nothing but a headache for them since the Quake..."

It was this that caused George Chan to gasp.

And both Lichen and Ragwort realized then that he'd been listening.

"Get away, Father!" cried Myrtle. But of course he couldn't hear her at all.

Ragwort, who was one of the Magic Isle's most powerful sorcerers, did an odd movement with his finger and, quite against his will, George Chan was being dragged over to them, his own body no longer under his own control.

"No!" cried Myrtle helplessly.

"Ah, Mr Chan, this is unfortunate," said Ragwort, almost pityingly.

Mr Chan struggled to fight his enchantment. "Stealing magic from someone else is banned!"

"Yes," said Lichen, toying with a fork.

"Shh, don't tell the head of the Banned Magic Office," said Lord Ragwort with a chuckle. "Oh, wait, I'm already here..."

"He's despicable," said Eglantine.

Arthur nodded.

Myrtle gasped, "Let him go!" forgetting that they were in a memory.

Eglantine reminded herself that they needed to see the curse to find out how to break it. The scroll was still on the table and her eyes were drawn to the first few lines...

Drawing Magic from Stone

Here exists a forbidden curse that the caretakers of this Grimoire should be aware of, as if used it can create a power never seen before...

She tore her gaze from the description of the curse, scanning the document for the part they needed, the counter-curse, but Lichen moved it out of eyesight.

"No!" cried Eglantine and Myrtle, as Lichen folded the paper and put it in his jacket pocket.

Eglantine tried to snatch it, but her hands passed through Lichen's jacket like she was a ghost.

"Since you're here, perhaps you can persuade my friend to see my point of view, Mr Chan? Nod if you understand," and George was nodding, but his eyes looked glazed.

"In order to achieve this miraculous piece of good fortune with this, yes, *banned* curse," continued Ragwort, "my friend here needs a bit of help, from me, to cast it properly. Which naturally I'm willing to do, but all I ask is for him to wait. For the autumn. So that I can put some other measures in place. We can't rush ahead. First we have to prepare the ground, so to speak."

"It's a creeping curse. It won't happen overnight, so I don't see why we have to wait."

"Because we can't do it before we start our campaign against magical creatures. We have to make everyone hate them, consider them a danger, so that by the time they turn to stone they're convinced it's for the best. If we do it too soon...well, people might start asking questions. Trying to find a cure."

"They can't do anything about it, though – not without the counter-curse," spat Lichen, patting his pocket where he'd put the spell.

"You don't know my sister," said Ragwort. "She's crafty. We cannot let her get wind of this. We can't make our move until we are sure she won't be able to stop us. If we do it too early, we give her the time to break it before the planets align on Halloween. She could still break it with the Witchlight, but if we wait till the autumn, there won't be long until it's permanent."

Eglantine gasped. She wasn't the only one. They all stared at each other in horror.

They had until Halloween to break the curse.

"So, Mr Chan, what do you say? Do you think my friend here should wait, as I advise, so that we can put our campaign in action before anyone gets the chance to use the Witchlight?"

He looked at Mr Chan expectantly, then chuckled. "My apologies," he said, then waved his fingers and George's eyes went clear. He was back in control of himself. He shook his head vehemently. "No, I DON'T. I don't think you should do this curse at all! It's wicked – you can't wipe out magical creatures just because dealing with them is a 'headache', as you put it. You don't get to decide who gets to live and who doesn't."

"See, now," said Lord Ragwort with a growing smile, "that's

where you're wrong. We've been deciding exactly that for some time now. Magic has led to many wondrous changes in our society," he said. "But, alas, for some, it has meant that our way of life has had to suffer, some changes have been too rapid. So I have taken it upon myself to slow it down, and even reverse some of those changes. We couldn't just kill girls with magic outright, unlike magical creatures who are simply a blight on our existence, girls have other uses to society. So we simply ensure that most girl children have their magic bound, as well as boys from, shall we say, less advantageous backgrounds, unless they show some promise we can utilize..."

Mr Chan gasped. "You've been *binding* their magic?"

Ragwort waved a hand. "It's simple enough. They think they're going in for the test, then..." He made a knitting sort of action with his fingers. "And once we are rid of these creatures, and we've put a lid on being progressive, we can go back to how things were. With magic in the hands of the people who were always meant to be in charge."

"You can't do that!" cried Mr Chan. "You can't wipe out magical creatures just because they are a threat to you, or turn back the clock so that girls don't get magic! Why would you even want to? My daughter is one of the smartest people I know, why should it matter what her gender is? Why should that or wealth or privilege or whether one is human or not determine who gets to succeed or *live*?"

Lichen scoffed. "Because that's the way it has always been. Those in charge make the rules."

Mr Chan shook his head. "Only if we allow people like you to get away with this."

Ragwort laughed.

"Oh dear. Shall I tell him, or will you?"

Mr Chan's eyes looked from Ragwort to Lichen.

The light in his eyes seemed to fade. He knew his fate then, before Ragwort said in mock sadness, "My dear fellow, it's you who will never get away."

Myrtle's face was stricken with horror.

"I think we should go now," said Eglantine gently to Myrtle, who was beginning to shake. She put an arm around her, then scrubbed the boot of her heel on the ground, and the strange shimmery light that had surrounded them began to dissipate.

They found themselves back on the pavement across from the burned-out building, inside the broken chalk circle.

It was just the three of them.

Mr Chan was gone. He'd left now that he had finally managed to warn someone about what he'd heard.

Eglantine held tightly to Myrtle as she sobbed onto her shoulder. Arthur patted her back.

Eglantine felt tears shimmer in her eyes. "He was brave, your dad," she said.

"Yes, he was," choked Myrtle.

"His death won't be in vain," promised Arthur fiercely.

"You're right," she said, pushing up her glasses, a determined look on her teary face, as she touched something in her pocket.

18
THE TRUTH CATCHER

Myrtle opened the door to her flat, then closed it behind her with a heavy heart.

Eglantine and Arthur had offered to stay with her, but she had declined.

What she wanted was to be alone.

She closed her eyes.

As soon as she did, her father's face flashed behind her eyelids.

They had toyed with him, and then they had murdered him.

A burning rage mixed in with her sadness. Hot tears slipped down her cheeks. She didn't know how to live with that.

From the corridor came the sound of soft padded footsteps.

"Myrtle, is that you?" came her aunt's concerned voice. A sparklight switched on to reveal her Aunt Ida, whose usually elegant bun was in disarray. There were dark circles beneath her kind eyes.

"I've been so worried! It's late. You've been out for hours! No note…" Her voice tailed off as she caught sight of Myrtle's face. "Oh, are you alright?"

This time, Myrtle couldn't find it in her to tell her aunt she was fine. She shook her head. "No, Aunt Ida," she said, and her shoulders began to shake as she let out the sobs she'd been holding back all night.

"Oh, my dear," said Ida, gathering her in an embrace. "Of course you're not. That's right, dear, let it all out."

After several cups of her aunt's sweet tea, Myrtle told Ida a little of what had happened. She couldn't tell her everything, not yet anyway (not when so much of it involved breaking the law – such as the fact that she had enrolled in a banned magical course, and joined an illegal society of witches), but she told her the important things. Like how she wasn't really coping with her father's death and the fact that he came back as a ghost to haunt his business, instead of to see her, had been a constant source of pain.

"But, Myrtle dear, that's just *not* true," said Ida with a look of surprise. "I thought you knew. We all see his ghost, but as soon as we approach, he vanishes. You're the only one he *waits* for. I think whatever it was he felt he needed to warn us about, he always meant it for you."

"Oh," said Myrtle, taking a sharp breath. Her chin started to shake again. "Oh."

She had felt that she had cried all she would that night, but her aunt's words caused fresh tears to slip down her cheeks.

She hadn't known that at all.

She swallowed, then thought back to what her father had said to those awful people who had killed him, how proud he'd seemed of his clever daughter, and how disgusted he'd been at the thought of them taking away her chance at getting magic.

Maybe her aunt was right. Maybe, out of everyone, he had wanted to warn her.

That evening, in her quiet attic bedroom that offered a distant view of the dragon bookshop and cafe on the corner, its amber lights winking like half-lidded eyes, Myrtle fed a fresh sheet of paper into her spark-typewriter.

She placed the tiny embroidery hoop, her truth catcher, onto her desk, and spoke the words that brought it to life.

And there, in her quiet room, came Lord Ragwort's cultivated voice.

She sucked in a breath of air.

When she'd activated it while they were inside her father's memory, she'd done it out of sheer hope that somehow, some way, it would recognize the truth and help her expose what Ragwort and Lichen had done, even though she was inside a memory.

And it had *worked.*

Lord Ragwort's voice brought chills down her spine, and fresh tears to her eyes as she listened...

"The fire at the Palace of Westminster took care of any link you and I had to the Whistlewitch and our plans to steal

Huswyvern, so there's no paper trail of our connection to that unfortunate bit of business... All I'm asking is that you be patient for a few more months, my dear fellow."

"Why wait, then?" said Lichen. Myrtle got goosebumps as she heard his voice. "Thanks to this curse I will be able to steal magic from magical creatures and homes..."

It was all *there*.

How they had enacted the curse on magical creatures and even how they'd bound the magic of children. And how they planned to murder her father.

She took a deep breath and began to write.

19
THE PLANETARY ALIGNMENT

It was dawn, several hours after Eglantine had witnessed Myrtle's father's last memory, and she woke up feeling panicked, as well as sad, tired and run-down. Her nose had started to stream. For weeks now she hadn't felt particularly well. But it was worse today. The ashy spot on the back of her neck had got bigger and her little arm had been aching for ages. Today it felt numb and hard to move.

She wondered if it was some kind of sympathetic response to what Hus was going through.

Or if she was sick from all the stress, especially after what she'd witnessed the night before, as well as what she had discovered.

She sat at the desk in her bedroom to write Miss Hegotty a speed-mail letter. They didn't have a moment to lose.

Dear Miss Hegotty,

Can you call an emergency society meeting for us, please? When we were inside George Chan's last memory we found out when the curse becomes permanent. It's on Halloween. In three days' time.

Eglantine

The magical mail was a useful trick that Miss Hegotty had taught them all. Especially for moments like these when time was of the essence. Or when you were worried about someone.

She couldn't stop thinking about Myrtle.

She sent her a speed-mail letter too.

Dear Myrtle,

I woke up thinking of you. I hope you're okay. I'm here if you want to talk about it, or even if you don't and you just want some biscuits and company while we figure out how to steal the counter-curse.

Eglantine

Myrtle's reply came moments later. Shortly after, their protection flowers showed that Miss Hegotty had called an emergency meeting.

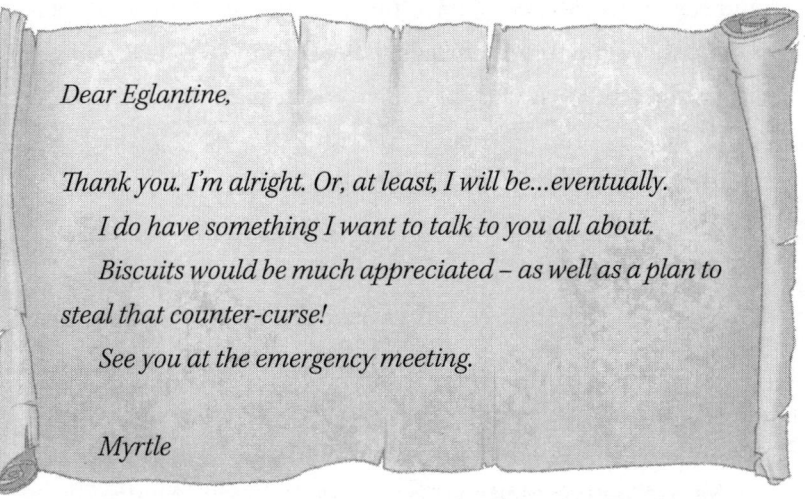

Dear Eglantine,

Thank you. I'm alright. Or, at least, I will be...eventually.
  I do have something I want to talk to you all about.
  Biscuits would be much appreciated – as well as a plan to steal that counter-curse!
  See you at the emergency meeting.

Myrtle

The emergency meeting took place an hour later. Eglantine, Arthur and Myrtle filled the others in on what happened.

It seemed everyone was on the same page.

"We should break into Lichen's place and steal the counter-curse today," said Eoin.

Everyone agreed, apart from Miss Hegotty, who shook her head. "We should wait. You've only been trailing him for a day. Let's get a better idea of his movements first – we just need to know what security he has in place, as we only have one chance to get this right."

They all reluctantly agreed.

"Shouldn't we expose them now though?" said Myrtle. "Now that we have the proof of what they've done?"

She had surprised them with the article she was writing and her truth catcher. "I have most of the proof we need," she said, fishing out the embroidery hoop from her navy pocket, and telling them about how her Witchspark allowed her to store the truth into objects.

There were sharp intakes of breath all around.

"You recorded the memory?" gasped Arthur, taking the truth catcher from her with a look of astonishment.

Everyone was talking enthusiastically, and exclaiming over the news.

"Lichen and Lord Ragwort could be arrested. Imagine that," breathed Miss Luthuli.

Miss Hegotty had been the only one to frown. "Myrtle, this is excellent work – and to have written it after everything you've been through is deeply admirable. But I think we should wait."

"What? Why?" cried Eoin.

"People need to know what they've done!" agreed Nandi. "We have the spark-staff now, so we can show them how it works, how they've been binding children's magic and thanks to Myrtle's truth catcher you have Ragwort and Lichen's confession! We could take this to your contact at the Department, Mrs Kusum, and her supporters who have been looking for a way to expose them."

"I don't deny any of that, and I agree – going forward with this is important. I will keep Mrs Kusum informed, but we cannot act on this yet: too much is at stake. Breaking the curse first must remain our focus. Right now, they don't know that we know about the curse, or that we're looking for the counter-curse. We cannot risk exposing them, and for Lichen to panic and do something regrettable."

Eglantine frowned. "Like what?"

"Like get rid of the counter-curse."

Myrtle gasped. "I never thought of that. You're right. He might do just that if he thought people were coming for him – try to get rid of any evidence."

"Exactly. Which is why we need to trail him properly and get a more detailed picture of his movements before we break inside his home or office and try to find the curse."

Miss Hegotty's eyes clouded over for a moment as she stared into the distance. "I have a sense of when the time will be right for us to break in – we have one chance to get this right. There is a particular moment when this will be clear for us to act; we have to wait for that. You have to trust me."

Two days had passed since that meeting and Miss Hegotty hadn't yet given them the go-ahead to break in.

Eglantine wasn't the only one who was getting desperate.

Miss Hegotty had asked them to trust her but tomorrow was *Halloween*. If they didn't act before midnight tonight the curse would be *permanent*.

Eoin had been talking of breaking in himself, and Arthur had taken to following after the boy to ensure he didn't do anything rash.

This morning, her copy of *The Weekly Spellcast* arrived. The headline read:

HISTORIC PLANETARY ALIGNMENT THIS HALLOWEEN!

She hadn't slept much the night before.

Why had Miss Hegotty left it this long for them to break in?

She started coughing and couldn't stop. Then she made her way miserably into the kitchen, where there was no sign of Tidbit.

She knocked on her cupboard.

It took an age before there was an answer and when she saw the gnome, Eglantine felt tears prick her eyes. She had got worse. Parts of her little body had turned completely to stone.

"Oh, Tidbit," she breathed. "I'm so sorry. We're going to break this curse."

Tidbit just stared at her. It was clear she didn't believe her.

Eglantine left the kitchen feeling helpless and frustrated and unbearably sad.

The flu-like symptoms Hus had been battling had mostly gone away – only to be replaced by a general ashy appearance, and for some of the rooms to have turned to stone. The mayhem was gone, but at least before Hus was fighting…

It was beginning to feel hopeless.

Arthur too had got worse, and he was out there with Eoin waiting for Miss Hegotty to send word that they could break into Lichen's home.

Her eye drifted to her protection flower, which she'd pinned to her cardigan, as Miss Hegotty had said it was best to ensure they had them on at all times, even when they slept, so that if they found themselves facing any danger, the society would be alerted.

Arthur had gone with Eoin for his evening patrol the night before. She hadn't heard him come in. She had a bad feeling. She wished Miss Hegotty would send a signal that it was time, before Eoin did anything that might put him and Arthur in danger out of desperation.

While she was worrying about them, and seeing Tidbit's doubtful face in her mind's eye every time she closed her eyes, she heard a letter arrive through the letter box.

It was from her father.

She put it in her pocket and then went to her mother's garden, where she tried to take her mind off the unsettled feeling in her stomach.

She often went to her mother's courtyard garden when she needed to feel calm. The plants that grew there were a riot of colour and variety that paid no attention to things like seasons or geography. In late October roses grew alongside hellebores, peonies and daffodils.

It was the place she often felt closest to her mother.

She sighed, took a seat and opened her father's letter.

Darling Eglantine,

It's rained every day since I've been here so I haven't got to see much, but what I have seen is green and beautiful. The good news is that it has allowed me to sort through much of the Welsh library as there has been little else to do but work.

The task you set me to assist you with academic research on "the history of magical creatures and any curses they may or may not have endured in the past and how they were broken" was surprisingly simple, only because in the whole of the library there was only one volume on the subject. It is called Magic Stone by Seraphine Kalk.

I have made a spark-paper copy of the relevant section, which I have included with this letter.

Your loving father,
Persicaria Bury

PS I hope that your interest in this subject truly is only academic – the section I have sent you is a bit worrying, considering your bond. You would tell me if anything was wrong, I hope?

PPS The biscuits were delicious. Sorry you risked life and limb for them.

PPPS That is very sweet about The Boots, but I do hope they aren't leaving mud on my bed.

PPPPS Please send Arthur and Hus my love.

Eglantine turned to the extract he'd sent her.
And the small smile vanished from her face.
Her heart raced as she read.

For years, scientists have tried to understand why magical creatures are impervious to illness. As I noted in my first book, The Creatures and Houses That Awoke from Stone, *in the early years after the Quake, it was legal to hunt magic creatures and take samples from magical homes.*

What has come out of these findings is that the only thing which appears to affect these formerly stone creatures and homes is magic – such as curses or magical bonds.

If a curse affects the witch, wizard, home or creature, both of the bonded pair will be affected, as a result of their union. Curses can manifest in the creature or home displaying what appear to be "flu-like" symptoms. If a counter-curse is not found, the result is a return to stone (or, in the case of a human bonded to a creature or sentient home, death).

Eglantine raised her hand to the spot on her neck.

She had thought it was stress, or some sympathetic response to Hus, but now she knew...

If they didn't find the counter-curse, she would die like the others.

20

A FLORAL WARNING

Eglantine made her way back inside. She felt a bit wobbly after reading her father's letter.

She didn't know why she hadn't realized it sooner.

The bond she shared with her magical home meant that if one suffered, the other would too.

It was why Hus had started to slowly die after Eglantine's mother passed. It had needed a new magical bond with a human or it would follow her to the grave...or in Hus's case, back into stone.

Something distracted Eglantine from the contents of the letter. The Boots were pacing up and down in agitation.

She frowned. The Boots only ever acted that way when Arthur was out...

"Is Arthur still not back?"

The coat rack wrung its spindle arms together in anxiety and shook its head, before pointing to a clock on the mantelpiece.

It was afternoon now. "He's been gone since last night," she said, frowning.

The coat rack nodded.

She sighed. "He'll be back soon," she said, feeling some of Hus's worry slide inside her heart. *Where was he?*

Just then her protection flower made an odd noise, and she realized in horror that the niggling feeling she and Hus had been experiencing all morning wasn't nothing at all.

Her protection flower glowed a dark red, and started to transform, switching continuously between two different plants. A clover and a snapdragon.

It was Eoin and Arthur.

And they were in danger.

21

THE BREAK-IN

Half an hour later, the headquarters of the Secret Society of Witches was in mayhem.

The protection flowers had revealed their friends' location. Eoin's clover and Arthur's snapdragon combined to form an attractive white house on a fashionable London street, lined with plane trees.

Lichen's house.

Victoria had arrived through her portal, clearly distraught. "Have you heard anything? Eoin has been so anxious – I was worried he'd do something like this!" she cried.

Soon after, Nandi and Miss Luthuli arrived, looking equally upset.

Myrtle, who had taken a lightning-carriage, arrived at the same time as Miss Hegotty.

"Did he catch them spying?" asked Myrtle. "Surely Eglantine's shawl-of-a-hundred-disguises would have helped?"

"I don't know. The flowers can only tell us that they are there, inside. Likely being held captive."

"I think Eoin was desperate to do something. He must have decided to break in and try to find the counter-curse, even though we told him to wait for Miss Hegotty's signal," said Victoria.

Miss Hegotty closed her eyes for a moment, shame flitting across her features, followed by a look of determination. She looked at them all. "The moment I was waiting for is now. For Eoin to act the way he did. It's part of the puzzle – they needed to be taken before we could follow."

Everyone stared at her in dismay.

"You were waiting for this?" exclaimed Eglantine in horror. "For them to be taken *hostage*? I can't believe you – we trusted you!"

Miss Hegotty looked pained. Eglantine saw now that the witch was pale and thin, her face tight. It was clear she was under strain, that she found this unbearable.

"I know. I am so sorry. But this was how it had to be, Eglantine. This was the only version of events in which I sensed we would be able to break the curse. Had we broken in earlier, the puzzle would have shifted..."

"We are not puzzle pieces. These are people's lives, Miss Hegotty!" snapped Victoria.

Miss Hegotty looked stricken. "I know that, Victoria, trust me.

Sometimes I *curse* this Witchspark I have," she said with genuine feeling. "But it's reliable. The way things fit together, if we had intervened earlier, the curse would have become permanent and there would have been…" She paused, and looked at them all meaningfully. "So many deaths."

Eglantine inhaled sharply. Despite her revulsion at what had happened, how Miss Hegotty had played her cousin like a pawn in a game of chess, she felt a stab of sympathy for the older witch. It wasn't like she *wanted* to.

She could see from how upset Miss Hegotty was that it wasn't a decision the witch had taken lightly.

"It's okay, you had to do it," said Nandi.

"Yes," agreed Miss Luthuli.

"It's not really okay, but thank you. I couldn't tell any of you what needed to happen or we might have prevented it," said Miss Hegotty. "There's too much at stake."

"We have to go after them now, though," said Eglantine. It was only worth it if they could save them and break the curse.

Miss Hegotty agreed. "Yes."

"I'm coming too," said Victoria. "I don't care if anyone panics that I'm gone, I can't just go home and wait to hear if Eoin or Arthur are alright."

They all nodded.

Miss Hegotty patted her left pocket, then her right, and opened it to reveal a tiny glass jar that looked completely empty.

"These are invisible barley sweets," she said. "They should last for around an hour. Eat up."

Miss Hegotty passed the jar around.

Eglantine frowned and stuck her fingers in the jar, surprised to find that something was definitely inside. She picked up an invisible sweet and popped it into her mouth. It tasted a bit like medicine.

The others did the same, turning to face each other in confusion.

"It hasn't worked! We're not invisible," said Victoria.

Miss Hegotty nodded. "Not to each other, no, but no one else can see us."

Then she adjusted her cloak, and said, "Follow me," as they went through the London portal.

They stood before the quiet house in Mayfair. It didn't seem like the kind of place where someone like Lichen would live. By rights, he should have been living on a hill in some turreted gloomy building.

Miss Hegotty consulted the watch that was pinned to her dark-blue striped dress, and drew up a hand for them all to wait.

It was four p.m.

"According to Eoin's patrols, Lichen should be leaving for his afternoon meeting now." They were hiding just outside the driveway.

Soon, the dark blue door opened, and Lichen came striding out, dressed in a dark-grey suit and hat.

Eglantine couldn't help recoiling when she saw him

approaching from the short walkway from the house.

There was a subtle transformation to him. He walked with heavier steps. He seemed more angular. Everything about him was more solid, weightier. As if his bones had taken on the characteristics of the formerly stone creatures and homes he'd been leeching magic from.

His eyes were an odd pale blue.

They watched him turn left.

"Alright," said Miss Hegotty after they'd watched him cross the street and disappear from sight. "It's safe."

"Did he seem different to you?" whispered Victoria.

"The magic has had an effect," said Miss Hegotty.

Eglantine nodded. It had, but the biggest change in her uncle wasn't the way he walked, or how pale his eyes were, it was the unusual expression on his face.

He was happy.

That's what frightened her most.

"How are we going to get in?" asked Eglantine.

"Simple," said Miss Hegotty, then rang the doorbell.

She put a rolled-up newspaper on the side of the mat furthest away from the door.

The others made to run and hide, but Miss Hegotty shook her head. "No one can see us, remember?"

"Oh, yes," said Myrtle and Nandi, letting out embarrassed chuckles.

The door was opened by an old man dressed in a butler's uniform. He was bald, apart from the grey hair on either side of his head. He had dark eyes with heavy shadows beneath them, and they widened in surprise to find an afternoon paper delivery.

Miss Hegotty beckoned for them to get inside as soon as the butler bent to retrieve the newspaper with a puzzled look on his face. They scuttled into the hallway.

When the butler turned to come inside and close the door, Victoria raised her hands and froze him in time.

They all breathed easier after that.

If the house outside was attractive and bright, the interior was dark and formal. The walls were painted a blue like the deepest part of the ocean, and the floors were black marble.

It was beautiful, in a cold sort of way, and perhaps inside one got more of a sense of the person Lichen really was.

There were no portraits on display. Just enormous, imposing statues of predatory animals. Like eagles and jackals.

They took quiet steps. Victoria looked around, in case they encountered anyone else on Lichen's staff.

When they rounded a corner, they saw an older woman in uniform admonishing a young girl for the way she'd lit a fire.

"Not like that, you silly girl! Put the cloth down first, Mabel. Sometimes, I swear someone replaced your brains with cotton wool."

"Yes, Mrs Hardwood," said Mabel hollowly.

Victoria stepped forward and froze them.

As they passed by Mabel, and her hangdog expression, Eglantine felt a sting of pity for the girl.

"Should we tie ol' *Hard*wood's bootlaces together?" whispered Nandi.

Miss Hegotty gave a wry smile. "Tempting, but best not. Somehow, I feel certain poor Mabel will get the blame."

But before they left, Miss Hegotty took a piece of paper from out of her jacket. It was one of the adverts for her course. "If anyone could do with finding her spark, it's you," she whispered, patting the girl on the shoulder.

Eglantine hoped that somehow she'd heard her.

The house was large, and the rooms were empty.

"They're definitely in the house," said Miss Hegotty, looking at her protection flower, which had changed from showing them the outside of the house, to what looked like a study.

They entered the room, hoping to find the others, perhaps restrained somewhere but close by. But the room was empty.

There was a large black desk topped with an assortment of writing paraphernalia, a feather quill and inkstand, a stack of fresh paper, a spark-typewriter, and a tarnished-looking decorative brass lamp. Along the back wall was a large cabinet and next to this, a bookcase.

"Perhaps there's a secret entrance in the bookcase?" said Myrtle. "I've heard about those, where you just need to pull the right book out," she said, then set about pulling almost all of them out.

Eglantine and Victoria opened the cabinet, but apart from

some files, it was empty.

"There's nothing here," said Nandi, looking under the desk.

Miss Hegotty was feeling along the wooden floor for a sign of a trapped door or a loose floorboard.

Eglantine created a set of giant watercolour dandelions, which scattered across the room, thinking that if their friends were also invisible, but tied up, they would touch against them. Nothing happened.

"They have to be here," said Miss Hegotty.

Victoria nodded.

Eglantine thought about how stark the rest of the house was. So free of any kind of decorations or mementoes, apart from the occasional bird of prey.

The brass lamp was the only thing she'd seen that could be described as ornamental, and yet it didn't quite match the rest of Lichen's things. It seemed out of place.

She picked up the lamp in curiosity, only to yelp. "It's hot!"

Miss Hegotty rushed over.

She touched it too, then gasped. "It's enchanted," she said with wide eyes.

"It reminds me," said Nandi, "of those stories, you know...with Aladdin and the magic carpet. Like if you rubbed it, a genie would come out."

They all turned to her and she looked embarrassed. "I'm just saying, that's what it looks like."

Eglantine studied the lamp again, then began to rub it, just as Miss Hegotty said, "Our instincts can surprise us."

Sure enough, two different hues of smoke began to curl from the spout of the lamp – one bright lime green, the other a dark emerald – and spilled out into the room.

22

THE COUNTER-CURSE

The smoke from the brass lamp transformed into the shapes of Eoin and Arthur.

They each had brass cuffs around their wrists.

Everyone rushed towards them, speaking at once. "Are you alright?" cried Eglantine.

"What happened?" asked Victoria.

"Did he hurt you?" breathed Myrtle.

Then, when there was no response...

"Arthur?"

"Eoin?"

But there was no sense of recognition from either of them.

"Can't they see us?" asked Eglantine. "Are the invisibility sweets still working?"

"I'm not sure," said Victoria. "But even if they were, they should be able to hear us."

"Nandi is right. It's like the story. Look on the lamp, see if there is anything written there, anything that activates them," said Miss Hegotty.

Eglantine picked up the lamp she had dropped on the floor in her shock. There was faint writing along the perimeter and she read it aloud.

WHATSOEVER IS HELD INSIDE GRANT ME THE POWER
TO COMMAND. WISHES THREE I ALONE SHALL DECIDE.

Suddenly, as one, Eoin and Arthur bowed, and turned to face Eglantine.

"That's a bit creepy," whispered Nandi.

It got worse, as they spoke as one.

"We are the genies from whom you may command wishes three. We cannot turn back time, bring someone back from the dead or kill. Or grant you more than your wishes three. So, think long over what is deep in your heart's desire. What shall it be?"

"They're trapped inside some kind of enchantment," cried Nandi.

Eglantine was staring at them both in horror, her heart in her mouth. She hated this.

"Is there any way to break it?" asked Eglantine.

"I'm afraid not," said a cheerful-sounding voice from behind, who snapped his fingers as he walked into the room. "That's better." He had somehow undone the invisibility magic of the barley sweets with a simple click of his fingers.

They all turned in shock.

Lichen had returned.

Victoria tried to use her magic to freeze him, but he grinned and batted off her magic as if swatting away a fly. "Was something supposed to happen, Your Royal Highness?" he asked with a wry smile.

Victoria swallowed and took a step back.

Eglantine quickly began to create a series of vines to throw over him like ropes, but these too were brushed away.

"I was looking forward to seeing you again, niece," he said, eyes glinting.

"That makes *one* of us."

Suddenly Nandi transformed before their eyes, taking on the shape of one of Lichen's birds of prey. She flew towards him, taking him by surprise. Miss Hegotty opened her coat and threw a glass jar at him. It shattered at his feet, and a large tidal wave swept him over.

"Quick, Eglantine, use your wishes!" she commanded.

Eglantine's eyes widened. Was this it? Could she use the power of the genies to end the curse?

"I wish for the curse Lichen has used to steal magic to be reversed!"

To her dismay, Lichen began to laugh. "You can't reverse curses, you can only break them."

The genies nodded. "Alas, it's true," they said as one.

"Then I wish for you to break the curse that Lichen has made."

The genies shook their head. "The only thing that will break his curse is its counter-curse."

Eglantine blinked. "Fine, then I wish to have the counter-curse that Lichen stole!"

And suddenly a piece of paper appeared in her hands. She yelled in triumph.

Lichen screamed, "NO!" and directed a wall of flames towards her.

The flames licked towards them at an alarming pace. Miss Hegotty made to counter it with water spells, but the flames did not die.

Victoria, Myrtle and the others tried to help with spells of their own.

"We're only managing to reduce the flames!" Nandi. "Why aren't they going out?"

Lichen laughed. "Because you are no match for my powers."

Nandi blanched.

"They're stolen powers!" shouted Eglantine.

"Don't get distracted by him. Carry on with your wishes, set them free, Eglantine!" croaked Miss Hegotty, who was beginning to tire as she desperately tried to keep the flames from reaching them.

It was clear they wouldn't be able to hold on for much longer.

Eglantine looked at the vacant-eyed genies, her cousin and her best friend, and then thought fast.

"I wish for my Uncle Lichen to take the place of Arthur and Eoin so that he is trapped as a genie instead."

"Noooooo!" cried Lichen. But he began to transform before their eyes. The brass bracelets dropped from Eoin and Arthur's wrists and they snapped out of their enchantment, just as the smoky form of Lichen was swept into the lamp. From within they could hear his voice. "This won't hold me for ever. I will grow stronger as time passes and when the curse is permanent, I will break free."

"We will make sure that never happens," promised Eglantine.

The lamp grew silent and the enchanted flames dissolved.

"Well done!" cried Miss Hegotty as the others rushed forward to greet Arthur and Eoin. "You will need to be careful with that lamp. Don't use your remaining wish unless you absolutely have to. The powers Lichen has been gaining will soon be much stronger than that of a genie enchantment."

Eglantine nodded. She didn't want to risk Lichen breaking free of the lamp the more powerful he became.

Eoin and Arthur were confused.

"What's going on?" said Eoin.

"What happened?" cried Arthur. "One minute we were inside his office, the next everything went dark."

"You don't remember?"

They shook their heads. Nandi rushed an answer.

"You have the counter-curse?" cried Arthur.

"Yes!" said Eglantine, holding her hand up to show them the scroll she was clutching.

They all gathered around to read it at last.

Drawing Magic from Stone

There exists a forbidden curse that the caretakers of this Grimoire should be aware of, as if used it can create a power never seen before…

They skimmed over the text until they got to the part about the counter-curse.

"The Witchlight *is* the counter-curse!" exclaimed Myrtle.

Counter-curse
Stars align to create the Witchlight

You will need six persons with magic in their veins (human or otherwise) to form a six-pointed star across the Isle and speak the counter-curse at the same time, before the planets align at midnight.

From sky above
To ground below
Knit our words to the bone

Together as one, we stand to put things right
To restore what was taken
We cast our mighty Witchlight
To return the magic that has been stolen
To reawaken the beasts from stone
With our words and our deeds
So, shall it be
Shine our light bright
We cast our mighty Witchlight

"Midnight? We have to do this tonight?" cried Victoria. "I still thought we had a day!"

Miss Hegotty winced and shook her head. "Technically Halloween begins at midnight tonight."

She checked her watch. "It's five o'clock. So we have seven hours to cast the Witchlight and break the curse."

That didn't sound long at all.

A strange sound outside made them startle. Eglantine and the others turned to the window that overlooked the street, where they saw a tall man hastening a retreat, his shoulders squared in a determined way.

Myrtle turned pale. They had been seen, and perhaps overheard.

"Was that...Lord Ragwort?"

23
ALL HALLOWS' EVE

Time wasn't on their side.

Ragwort knew they had the counter-curse and there was no telling what he would do to prevent them from using it.

They hurried back to headquarters, only to discover how dire things were. Hus's magic was fading fast.

Arthur called out to The Boots, who usually knocked him off his feet in their excitement at his return.

They heard a soft thump. Like a dog that was trying to wag its tail but didn't have the strength.

"Boots?" whispered Arthur.

Eglantine breathed in sharply as she saw them, lying on their side under the table.

Arthur rushed towards them. Eglantine felt her throat turn thick with emotion.

The coat rack shuffled towards her as if it were wading against a tide.

"Oh, Hus," breathed Eglantine. "You're losing magic even faster now, as the curse strengthens."

The coat rack nodded.

She heard Arthur sniff as he picked up The Boots, and she saw to her horror that her friend was the same.

"Arthur," she whispered.

All the green of his scales had gone. He was getting worse by the minute the closer they got to the curse becoming permanent; he looked wan and grey.

He was fading fast too.

"They'll be okay," said Arthur, not realizing she meant him.

Eglantine had to fight the urge to break down in sobs.

Suddenly Eoin gasped. "Eglantine," he breathed, and she thought he was turning to her to comfort her, but she realized when she looked up at him that he was looking at her the same way she'd just been looking at Arthur. His face was stricken. "Your arm... It's..." he gasped. "It's turning..." He swallowed heavily and closed his eyes. When he opened them again he looked *devastated*. "Why didn't you tell us?" he said in a choked voice. "We're family."

Eglantine reached for his hand, but he turned away.

"Eoin!' said Victoria in surprise, only to gasp when Eglantine turned towards her. She saw now why Eoin was so upset.

Eglantine's little arm had turned to stone.

"Oh, no," whispered Victoria, clapping a hand over her mouth.

"I didn't want to worry you," said Eglantine, looking from her to Eoin.

"Well, you should have," he said, reaching for her hand and holding on tight.

Victoria rushed towards her other side, touching her little arm tenderly, her eyes, too, pooled with tears. "But why is it turning to stone? I don't understand."

"Milady?' breathed Arthur, looking up from The Boots.

"It's...the bond. If Hus dies, so do I."

The expression in Arthur's eyes almost caused her to fall apart, right then.

Eglantine folded her lips as she tried not to cry.

She looked around her, then took a deep breath. "I only found out this morning myself."

Arthur had tears in his eyes. "I hate that it's happening to you too. It feels worse somehow."

"Now you and Hus know how *I* feel," said Eglantine.

Eoin wiped his eyes, then looked from Eglantine to Arthur and nodded, and set his jaw. "Right, what are we waiting for? We have a curse to break!"

It was the rallying cry they were waiting for.

Sorcerer Nelson clearly agreed. He raised his sword slowly, like it took some effort. "You heard the lad! Charge!"

Miss Hegotty nodded. "Indeed. But first we need a map."

Then she looked at Victoria in a way that made Eglantine feel a stab of fear for her friend.

Eglantine realized that Victoria was also in danger. She had been gone from the palace for hours. "Victoria," she said gently. "By now your family must be very worried about you. No one would blame you if you went back through your portal. You were incredibly brave to come out and try to save Eoin. We have seven people, even without you, so you don't need to do this."

Victoria shook her head violently. "I do, Eglantine. I can't just go home and wait and hope that three of my best friends don't turn to stone. I can't live in fear any more that someone finds out I have magic and kicks me and my family out of our home or decides I am no longer fit to become queen. You know, if there's anything I've learned from you, and how you go through life, it's if they can't accept me, then maybe they don't deserve me."

Eglantine rushed forward to give her friend a hug. "Too right," she said. "In that case, help me find a map," she added with a grin, and together they rushed to Eglantine's father's study to fetch a map of the Magic Isles, so that they could draw their six-pointed star.

There was, to be expected, much debate about the location of where they needed to draw their six-pointed star. "Durness, I think," said Myrtle.

"No, Kirkwall is further up," said Eoin.

"Yes, but it's not in the centre—"

"I don't think it needs to be an exact science. In fact it would be best if it *wasn't*," said Miss Hegotty. "It'll be safer, as Ragwort and his corrupt Department could be placing lookouts there now.

"So long as the shape is recognizable, the magic will travel, creating the Witchlight."

It took them a good half-hour but eventually they had each of their points across the Magic Isles, from Scotland into Ireland, Wales and England.

It was decided that Myrtle would go to Tongue, in Scotland; Eoin to Galway in Ireland; Arthur would go to St David's in Wales, as he said the Welsh were far more tolerant about flying-dragon creatures; and in England, Nandi and Miss Luthuli would go to Plymouth. Victoria would go to London and Eglantine would go to Southwold. It was a wonky star indeed.

Miss Hegotty had a destination all of her own.

"It's time I faced my half-brother. Ragwort knows that we are on to him and his plans," she said. "I have to stop him from trying to sabotage us at all costs," she said.

"You can't face him on your own! I'll go with you. Nandi is more than capable of performing her part of the star alone," said Miss Luthuli.

Miss Hegotty shook her head. "My brother has tried and failed to capture me before. He is strong, but I have always been stronger, something he hates me for. I think you should be prepared, in case you need to take one of the others' places," she said, looking momentarily at Eglantine, then Arthur, with concern.

This caused everyone to look sombre.

Both Eglantine and Arthur were slowing down, but they were determined to do their part.

"Okay," said Eoin, nodding. "But how are we going to get where we need to go in time. Lightning-carriage?"

"Ragwort could monitor those," said Myrtle.

Miss Hegotty's eyes sparkled. "You're right. I think it's time for broomsticks."

There were gasps all around.

"As in, actual flying broomsticks?" breathed Eoin.

"But they're on the Banned—" began Arthur.

"*Don't say it*," they all cried, and he stopped, just in time.

"They are," agreed Miss Hegotty. "Although I'm assuming you'll prefer to fly yourself, Arthur?" she asked.

"Yes, thank you."

"Suit yourself," said Miss Hegotty. She patted down her coat, and pulled out a silk handkerchief, which she placed on the table and opened it to reveal what looked like several tiny, dried twigs.

"Um?" said Eoin.

Miss Hegotty winked. "Have a little faith, Eoin Murphy."

She stood and walked around the table.

"I would suggest getting out of your chairs," she said. "Then take one."

They followed her instructions, and each chose one of the twigs.

As soon as Eglantine's fingers touched hers, the twig grew warm, and revealed itself before her eyes.

"Your touch is like water," said Miss Hegotty. "Bringing it to life."

Eglantine's mouth fell open in amazement. Her twig had turned into a classic-looking broomstick. Well, almost. It was sleek and long, but instead of only twigs at the broom-end, there were also all sorts of flowers, including her namesake, eglantine.

It was beautiful. "Oh, thank you, Miss Hegotty," she breathed.

Victoria was staring at her broomstick in awe. It shimmered translucent, and appeared to fade away before her eyes, perfect for a princess who needed to hide the fact that she had magic.

Eoin's was a sleek racing green, with two golden stripes down the side.

Myrtle's looked somehow like a black-and-brass typewriter that had turned itself into a broomstick. "There is even a spot for my portfolio!" she said, drawing out a secret shelf in delight.

Miss Luthuli's looked like it was covered in moss, and could easily be camouflaged inside one of her greenhouses.

Nandi's was perhaps the most colourful. It looked a little like a multi-hued candy cane. "It's all my favourite colours," she said, doing a bit of a jig on the spot.

Miss Hegotty's was a smoky blue, and like Victoria's it blended into the shadows.

"They respond to you, and will only fly well for the witch or wizard it is made for. They have been enchanted with a direction spell, so once you tell your broom where you are headed, it will point you straight."

Eglantine sagged in relief at *that* news.

"Thank heavens," said Miss Luthuli, who clearly felt the same. "The thought of getting lost, now...*well*..." She looked at Eglantine, and then Arthur, her face grim.

No one had to say how important it was that they got to where they needed.

"At quarter to midnight, I will, all being well, send the signal that we should perform the spell. Your protection flowers will resemble a spellbook," she said, waving her hand over hers, and all of the protection flowers turned into tiny grimoires.

"The curse came with a warning against copying it down. It disappears as soon as you try, so I would memorize it now," she continued.

They spent the next while doing just that.

Suddenly there was a whining sort of sound from Hus.

The spark-typewriter tried to type something but the keys jammed.

Pns

"*Pns?*" said Nandi, staring at the spark-typewriter in some confusion.

The coat rack pointed at the London door.

Eglantine got up, and went to see, and found that the London door now had a keyhole, just like Victoria's portal did.

"Do you mean pins?" she asked.

The coat rack nodded. Then fell over, and didn't move any longer at all.

They stared at in horror.

"Oh, no!" cried Victoria.

There were cries of confusion and panic. "What's happening?"

Eglantine felt her heart twist in love for her beloved home. "You're using all your energy for this, Hus?"

She saw several iron pins jump up and down, making a tapping sound on the ground.

"That's what happened when Hus made my portal. My pin was tapping too," Victoria breathed.

"Oh!" gasped Eglantine. "Is that what you're doing, Hus, making portals for us to get back here?"

There was an answering thrum beneath her feet.

Then the spark-typewriter slowly and laboriously began to type again.

Pt n grnd, prtl apr.

It took a while, but Myrtle was the one who guessed what Hus meant.

"Put in ground, portal appear?"

One of the typewriter keys clacked.

"Y"

It was clear Hus didn't have its usual strength.

Eglantine gave the walls an affectionate pat. "I think Hus wants to make sure that if anything happens, we can get home safe. I think if it could, it would create portals to each of the points in the map for us, but that would take too much magic."

"It's okay, Hus. This is more than enough, thank you," said Eoin, and they all agreed, patting the walls the way they often saw Eglantine do.

Then it was time.

They had five hours to cast the Witchlight.

"What happens if someone gets into trouble?" asked Eoin. "Should we go and help?"

Miss Hegotty frowned. "Yes, if you feel you can get there and back to your destination in time. So, bear in mind who is where. There's no point all of us rushing in to help if it means you won't be able to get back to your location in time."

They all nodded. That made sense.

Miss Hegotty turned to leave through the London door.

Eglantine gathered with the others in the garden.

"Good luck," everyone called, as they climbed onto their new broomsticks.

Eglantine was the last to depart. She watched as they went, then readjusted her backpack so she could be sure the contents were safe. Inside it was only one item. The genie lamp containing Lichen. She took it with no intention of using it. Even stuck inside the lamp he was growing ever more powerful. There was the chance that if she rubbed the lamp she might not be able to command him to go back in. She would only consider using her last wish if it seemed like she had no other choice.

She climbed aboard her broom, and took a deep steadying breath, as she felt the smooth, glossy handle beneath her hand. Usually she would have been able to support herself with her little arm too, but she had no feeling whatsoever in it. She used her magic to create vines to tie her stony little arm to the broom.

Then she whispered her destination, and as she rose up from the ground, she saw Arthur disappearing into the horizon towards Wales.

Eglantine bit her lip.

Earlier, it had seemed like plenty of time to get across the country, but now, it felt like they would be rushing against the clock.

She closed her eyes for a beat, as she rose higher and higher into the air and began to move forward at pace.

It was different to riding with Arthur, where she felt in very safe talons; this felt...mildly terrifying.

She gasped when the broom shot forwards.

But being the one to steer it meant that, unlike the jostling of the lightning-carriage, she didn't feel sick.

Well, not as much.

Eglantine was just approaching the town of Southwold, when her protection flower began to whine and flash red. It showed a violet in danger.

Victoria.

Then it flashed to show her location.

She stared at her protection flower in shock. Victoria was supposed to be at her location in London. So why was she at the palace?

Something must have happened.

She came in to land on the beach in Southwold and thought hard.

The others were travelling much further. She was closest to London, apart from Miss Hegotty, who was likely preoccupied...

Could she could go and help and still get back in time to cast the Witchlight? What if she put the portal pin down into the ground here in Southwold, so that she could get back inside Huswyvern, and from there use Victoria's portal to get inside the palace? She looked at her watch. She had under three hours.

It was enough time. It would have to be.

She placed the portal pin in the ground and a shimmering door appeared out of nowhere. She was careful to leave the pin in place in Southwold so she could get back.

When she stepped inside Hus, she could feel it was panicking.

The floor lifted slightly towards where the doorway to Victoria's portal usually was.

Eglantine turned, and prepared to break into Kensington Palace.

24

The Other Portal

Eglantine peered through a gap in the wardrobe door.

Her eyes searched the room. She was about to push the door open, when she saw a pair of brown eyes staring back at her.

Eglantine swallowed.

The door shot open, and Eglantine found herself being pulled into the sitting room by a determined older woman with a severe parting in her hair.

"W-wait, I can explain," cried Eglantine, as she stumbled forward.

"There's no time," she said.

"N-no, please, you don't understand!"

"I do," said the woman, her face urgent. "You have to help her – help Victoria!"

Eglantine blinked. "That's why I'm here."

"Good!"

Eglantine blinked. She recognized her.

"You're...Lehzen?" she said, remembering that she had met her the year before, when Victoria's family had come to visit as part of their royal tour.

"Yes, Lady Eglantine," she said in greeting.

Eglantine frowned.

"You were expecting me?" she said. It wasn't like she had *planned* to break into the palace via Victoria's doll cupboard.

Lehzen looked stressed. "Not you, specifically. Although, come to think of it, I'm not all that surprised that it is you she meant. Ever since we met you last year, strange things keep happening, gaps in people's memories...but we don't have time to get into any of that now! Victoria is in trouble! She told me someone might be coming through the doll cupboard to help – I thought she was talking gibberish, but she made me promise to check, and...well! Here you are!"

"What's happened?"

"She was escorted back here half an hour ago by half of the Royal Isle-Spark Military, as if she were some kind of criminal. They're saying she was flying a broomstick in daylight in London! They're talking of charging her with treason."

Eglantine gasped. Ragwort had brought in the *military*. "Treason?"

Lehzen nodded. "It's mad. They said something about her having illegal magic... Conroy is trying to intervene."

Eglantine tried to take all this in.

"You mean he's trying to *help* her?"

"Yes," said Lehzen. Though she too looked a bit doubtful.

"But how did Ragwort find her? We took precautions!"

Lehzen frowned. "You mean it's true – she *was* somewhere, flying a broomstick?" she exclaimed. "When this is all over, Victoria and I are going to have a proper talk about how careless and irresponsible she has been. But first we need to save her. The only trouble is, I don't know how you will do it without your magic."

Eglantine looked at her in confusion. "What do you mean save her without magic?'

"The guards installed a device that blocks magic."

Eglantine closed her eyes for a beat. She had forgotten that.

"Maybe we can disable it?"

"It's with Ragwort, so you'd have to go through him."

"Okay," said Eglantine. "If we have to do that, I will."

Lehzen looked shocked.

"No offence, but how is one young girl meant to take on half the RISM and one of the most powerful sorcerers in the Magic Isles without magic?"

Eglantine looked at the governess. She had a point. Even without the curse to contend with, even *with* her magic, she wasn't strong enough to take them on by herself.

But she wasn't by herself. "There's something that might help."

Using the lamp might mean that Lichen got free, but she would take that risk if it meant she could save Hus, Arthur and others like herself from turning to stone.

Lehzen didn't seem convinced, but she said, "I hope so, for all our sakes. Come on." She led her from a handsome sitting room. Eglantine couldn't help gawping as they walked. She had never been inside a palace. The rooms were beautifully furnished, with expensive carpets and furniture. But they didn't have time to linger as they made their way down the stairs and towards the back of the palace, near the kitchens. It was oddly quiet, with no one around.

Eglantine said, "I know we don't have time to get into everything, but I want you to know that Victoria wasn't being irresponsible. She had a good reason for being where she was. She's been very brave."

Lehzen looked back at her in exasperation. "Lady Eglantine, if my girl manages to get out of this without going to prison, perhaps that will comfort me some day, but right now, I could cheerfully throttle her."

Then her face softened. She stopped and she put a hand on Eglantine's shoulder, and said, "I am grateful that you are here, though."

Suddenly her eye fell on Eglantine's little arm, and she looked concerned. "Are you alright? Your arm has turned grey."

Eglantine nodded. "It's another long story. I'm fine, or at least, I will be."

Perhaps it was the adrenaline coursing through her veins, but all she could feel was the importance of rescuing Victoria and returning to cast the Witchlight as quickly as possible.

Lehzen took her down a set of stone stairs. It was dark and cold and damp.

When they reached the bottom, she saw that they were in a basement. "It's where we house prisoners," whispered Lehzen.

Eglantine exhaled sharply. She couldn't believe they had brought Victoria *here.*

There were no windows, and low sparklights on the stone walls. In the shadows, they could see a hazy group of people sitting at a table. Beyond that, she could make out what looked like iron bars but the rest was shrouded in darkness.

A woman was sobbing loudly.

"There, there, this will all be over soon, Your Grace," said a rather cheery voice that caused the hackles to rise on Eglantine's neck. Lord Ragwort.

As they approached, a voice said sharply from the shadows. "Halt! State your business."

Several RISM officers stepped out of the shadows. They were followed by three royal guards, in their distinctive palace uniforms.

"I am Lehzen, Victoria's governess, we wish to see her—" she said.

"We?" said Lord Ragwort's voice eagerly. A light appeared by the table, and Eglantine could see him clearly.

She felt her legs wobble slightly in fear. He was sitting with his legs crossed at the ankle, reclining in his chair, looking very relaxed.

As the light fell on Eglantine, Ragwort guffawed in amusement.

"Oh, this is too much."

He was sitting next to Victoria's mother, who was weeping uncontrollably. Opposite her was Sir Conroy, who appeared similarly amused. "An entire illegal society of witches and this is who they send as your saviour, Princess? If I were you, I'd be wondering if it was worth the risk, if this is how they repay you..." He laughed, and Eglantine spotted Victoria in the cell behind them.

She was sitting on the stone floor, her arms locked in a set of spark-manacles. She thrashed against them, but when she saw Eglantine, she threw back her head defiantly, and glared at Ragwort. "Shows what you know, Ragwort. Eglantine is the strongest person I know."

He snorted.

"You have no right to imprison her like this!" cried Eglantine, racing forward.

Lord Ragwort sighed. "Actually, we do."

Eglantine didn't want to but she couldn't see another way. There were too many of them and she didn't have her magic.

They only had a few hours left before the curse became permanent.

She took off the backpack, then brought out the lamp, which she began to rub.

"I'll get you out of this, Victoria!" promised Eglantine.

"Eglantine, are you sure?" She had seen what she was about to do. "You heard what Miss Hegotty said," shouted Victoria.

"It's the only way."

She rubbed and she rubbed. But the lamp remained cold in her hand.

She felt a prickle of fear.

It wasn't working.

There was a loud snort from Ragwort. "The royal guards have installed a device that blocks human magic in the palace, so of course your little powers won't work, *tsk tsk*, but I have also added an extra precaution with this..." he said, waving his hand to where she could see a metal object on the table. "I had a small premonition I might need this today," he chuckled, "it's similar to the Eclipse but this one specifically blocks genie magic. A lucky guess one might say," he said, snorting.

Eglantine paled.

She could well understand why he'd thought to bring *that* today – after he'd witnessed Lichen being bound into the lamp earlier that afternoon.

"None of your little tricks will work here." He gave a wry smile.

Next thing she knew, Ragwort was out of the chair, and had taken the lamp from her hand. "Thank you," he said. "I was looking for this. You will get out shortly, old friend, just a few more hours and then nothing will be able to hold you."

From within the lamp they heard triumphant laughter.

Eglantine felt her blood run cold. She was completely outnumbered.

"This girl is right!" shouted the Duchess. "You have no right to imprison Victoria. I have heard what you said, and yes, I saw the broomstick – when you brought her in and put her in that cell, like some common criminal. But you MUST be wrong! I would know if she had magic. We have a very strict system. Victoria is never out of my sight!"

Lord Ragwort sighed. "Oh, my dear, children are clever creatures and while they do annoy me so, we don't give them nearly enough credit for their capacity to hoodwink their parents." He looked at Victoria and winked. "I'm afraid all your dark deeds are coming out now, my girl." He turned back to the Duchess. "Alas, Your Grace," he said, "not only does she have magic, she also has a very illegal type of magic, known as a Witchspark. This is a sorcerer skill. Very powerful indeed. Particularly hers, as it allows her to manipulate time." He tapped the lamp. "She was witnessed using it last year."

Eglantine and Victoria gasped, then looked at each other in realization. Lichen had told him.

Ragwort continued, "It appears she has been using these dark skills of hers on all of you. Have you not wondered at all the odd things that have happened over the past year? Odd pockets of time lost, food suddenly turning stone cold, hours passing in a blink of an eye…"

There was a sharp intake of air from Lehzen, as well as the Duchess, who clapped a hand on her mouth.

"Yes," nodded Ragwort. "That was your child. Not as innocent as she seems. Especially when she was freezing you in time for hours, laughing at you all, while she skipped off and enjoyed herself."

"No!" cried Victoria. "That's not true, Mother! I didn't enjoy it."

Her mother let out a faint squeak. She looked stricken.

"It's true?"

Victoria was crying now. "I had to, Mama."

Her mother blinked.

"*Tsk tsk*," tutted Ragwort. "You see what I mean. She concealed the fact that she has powers – for, am I right, Kang Mal-Chin? – over a year?"

The royal guard nodded. "We believe so, yes."

Victoria looked at the guard in shock. "You knew?"

Ragwort scoffed. "Give them some credit, Princess. We suspected even before Lord Lichen told us he'd witnessed you using your powers, despite the fact that you went to great lengths to hide it, using illegal spells and products to alter the memory of everyone in your household. You had your chance to come clean, but you chose the ungovernable path, and now you must face the consequences."

"I...I don't know how to deal with any of this," said the Duchess brokenly.

"There is a way," said Sir Conroy. "A way we can all go back to normal. Forget this ever happened."

The Duchess looked up hopefully. "There is?"

"Oh, yes," said Ragwort. "We've been in secret negotiations over this for weeks, trying to find a solution to this mess. As prime minister I can cut a deal with Victoria, so to speak."

"A deal?" breathed the Duchess, clinging to the words in hope.

Eglantine cried, "No! You don't want any dealings with this man – he is a criminal and a murderer. We can prove it!"

"Lies," said Ragwort. "Put that girl in chains; she has broken almost as many laws as the princess."

"No," cried Eglantine as several officers came forward to put her in chains.

"Sad, really," Ragwort continued. "You see, Your Grace, both girls are under the influence of the notorious Miss Hegotty."

"Miss Hegotty?" cried the Duchess. "The outlaw-witch?"

Ragwort nodded. "The very same. It's a long story, but they fell for her lies and enrolled in her banned course."

"No," breathed the Duchess.

"I can explain," cried Victoria, as Eglantine shouted, "Miss Hegotty isn't who the Department says she is – she's right, everything she says is right."

"Oh dear," said Ragwort again. "You hear them? Brainwashed. Completely brainwashed. You mustn't blame yourself, dear Duchess. Miss Hegotty has many tricks. That ungovernable thorn in my side has been influencing the minds of vulnerable children, making them believe all sorts of preposterous things. That we are somehow 'binding' children's magic, and this new one, that we're stealing magic from a bunch of mindless, dangerous creatures who unfortunately are just nearing the end of their life cycle. They're just sick and turning back to stone. It's sad, of course, but it's no one's fault. It's a blessing in a way, though. But it's hardly our fault…"

"It is, you liar! And they are not mindless beasts! They are far wiser than you," cried Eglantine.

Ragwort rolled his eyes. "Don't mind her, I believe she has one as a pet. "Enough. You see, Your Grace, how these children have been influenced by Miss Hegotty and her dangerous discourse? If anything, Victoria is a victim, and we can make it so that the law takes that into account. Especially now, in such exceptional circumstances, the people of the Magic Isles will need us to have a better solution than locking away the person who as of today would be hailed as queen."

"What? What do you mean?"

"It's my sad duty to announce that just before we found Victoria flying on a broomstick…we heard that the king had died—"

Everyone gasped.

"What? When?" cried Victoria, clapping her hand to her mouth.

The Duchess gasped. "It can't be. The poor man."

There were sudden tears in Victoria's eyes.

"A tragedy, of course," said Conroy.

"How…how did he die?" exclaimed Victoria.

"A fire, earlier this evening, apparently."

"No!" cried Victoria.

She and Eglantine shared a look of horror.

Eglantine whirled to face Ragwort. "Did you kill him too?" she cried, thinking of the fire at the Palace of Westminster and the one at Myrtle's father's pub.

"Don't be ridiculous. It was a horrible accident."

Then he turned to the Duchess. "Your Grace, it is in light of this tragedy that we must make alternative plans. Alas, with

Victoria clearly suffering under a delusion that the Department is the 'enemy', she is not fit to rule. It is my duty to look after the best interests of our country and to broker a deal that will ensure stability. The past has shown us a way forward when a monarch is unable to do their job. We can appoint someone. That can be you, Your Grace, you can become regent – and rule in Victoria's place. That way we can conceal all that has happened here. You can go back to living as before, the Eclipse will ensure she cannot use her powers, and you could add other protocols to keep her safe…

"All you would have to do is sign this document. Victoria would have to sign too, appointing you as regent. Then it will be as if this unfortunate mess never happened," he said, taking a piece of paper from his jacket pocket.

"No," cried Victoria and Eglantine together.

"It's a trick," cried Victoria.

The Duchess shook her head sadly. "Release her. I will sign and make sure Victoria does too," she agreed.

"Very well," said Ragwort, placing the document on the table, and handing her a pen. Then he snapped his fingers and one of the guards opened up the cell with Victoria.

"What about the other girl?" asked the Duchess.

Ragwort looked at Eglantine, who was being held by the guard, his eyes taking in her stone arm. He sighed. "I don't think she will be a problem much longer."

The Duchess looked confused, then nodded and began to sign the document.

"No, you can't do this, we have to get out of here!" cried Victoria. "They've put a curse on magical creatures, one that is affecting Eglantine too. If we don't help her, she will turn to stone – that's what he means. He's evil, Mother."

The Duchess's hand stilled. She looked over at Eglantine and saw how her arm was grey. She hesitated.

"It's nonsense," said Conroy. "Carry on. Together we can rule—"

"We?" said the Duchess, looking at Conroy oddly.

"I meant *you*. I would help you in whatever way you need, that's all."

The Duchess looked doubtful.

"He's lying," cried Eglantine. "He's been lying to you for months, scheming with his friend. Now they've figured out a way for him to rule – he thinks he can do it through you."

"Don't listen to the child," snapped Ragwort. "Sign, Your Grace."

"That would be a mistake," said a voice from behind. A voice that had appeared from nowhere.

It was a voice that gave Eglantine hope.

Miss Hegotty!

25

THE BOND

"Hello, brother."

Everyone whipped around, trying to see her, but they couldn't. She was *invisible*.

The smug smile was gone from Ragwort's face.

"Get her," he cried, and officers and guards dashed around the basement trying to find her.

There was the sound of laughter.

Ragwort paled.

"How are you doing this?" he cried. "We've enabled the Eclipse. Even your magic can't work against it!"

"Oh, brother, the trouble with you is that you always thought that my greatest skill was magic, when really it has been the ability to outsmart you."

Ragwort's face turned puce.

"That's not true – you've been on the run for years."

"Thwarting you at every turn, and soon exposing you for the liar, thief and murderer that you *are*."

He jerked around, trying to snatch at the air.

"You will never *prove* anything."

"Oh, but, you see, you are wrong – again," she chuckled. "I suspected you might attempt to kill the king. Which is why I paid him a visit shortly before you did and had him listen to your confession, recorded without your knowledge, where you admitted to binding children's magic, setting fire to the Palace of Westminster, promising to help Lord Lichen cast a curse that would eliminate magical creatures. Not to mention killing the innocent pub owner who overheard you. After that it was easy for me to convince the king to let me place a glamour spell on his home and let you *think* you had set fire to it and killed our reigning monarch. The truth is, he is fine. The same, however, cannot be said for you, brother."

Ragwort blanched. "The king is alive?"

"Alive and well!" cried a strident voice, coming into the dungeons. It was the king himself accompanied by his personal guards.

There were gasps all around.

Miss Hegotty whispered in Eglantine's ear, "The king's guard is powerful, but none of them can use their magic to fight Ragwort yet, so I need you to restrain him, Conroy and the RISM, before I disable the Eclipse. You may need to restrain the palace guards too, if they remain loyal to Ragwort."

"What?" whispered Eglantine. "But I can't use my magic!"

"Yes, *you* can, Eglantine. Think why the curse is working on you."

Eglantine frowned, and suddenly she understood what the witch meant.

Thanks to the bond she shared with Hus, she was also affected by the curse they had placed on magical creatures and homes... but that meant her magic wasn't like human magic – not completely. So the Eclipse device wouldn't work on her...there was a part of her, the part bonded to Hus, that wasn't human at all. It meant her magic might work here, just as Hus's did!

She took a deep breath and felt for her magic. It was not as strong and vibrant as it usually was, but it was there, flickering with life. She couldn't believe she hadn't noticed it before.

She focused on that, gritted her teeth and concentrated hard. Pushing past a rush of fatigue, she began to create a series of floral vines which she shot out towards Ragwort, tying him in place.

Ragwort yelped. "What! What is going on? How are you doing this? I thought of everything!"

Clearly, he had not.

Eglantine ignored him, a cold sweat breaking out on her forehead. A patch of skin by her cheek turned to stone as she concentrated on placing more and more ropelike vines around him.

"Help her," shouted the king. "Bind Ragwort's men."

Kang Mal-Chin and the other royal guards turned to help fight the RISM officers. It was ten against five.

Even so, one of Ragwort's men tackled her to the ground, and Eglantine felt the wind knock out of her, as the man held her down. She closed her eyes and concentrated hard. Suddenly an enormous, monstrous venomous flytrap appeared and swallowed him whole.

She saw the genie lamp had fallen near Ragwort, who was struggling against the vines she had bound him with. She shoved it inside her backpack just as Victoria rushed to her side, having been freed by a member of the royal gaurd.

"Come on," she said. "We have to go. Miss Hegotty and the king have them – they won't get out of this."

Eglantine hesitated, until she heard Miss Hegotty's voice say, "Ragwort, Conroy and Lichen are the ones going to prison, Eglantine, I promise you that – but now it's up to you two to break the curse. Go!"

26

TURNING TO STONE

There wasn't long until the curse would become permanent.

Victoria found her broom outside the steps of the basement. Someone must have put it there for her. Miss Hegotty, they thought.

"Thank you for coming to save me," said Victoria, squeezing her hand as she made her way to the kitchen door, ready to take flight.

"Any time."

They smiled at each other.

"Right. Well, let's break this curse, shall we?"

"That might be a good idea."

And then both girls set off for their destinations. Eglantine placed the backpack back over her shoulder and raced upstairs as fast as she could to the doll cupboard, only to find herself stumbling over her feet. She looked down in horror to find that her left leg had turned to stone. She had to drag it behind her as she made her way through the cupboard and into Hus.

Where she found that, like her, the house was fading fast.

"Quick, Hus, open the door to where my portal pin in Southwold is!"

It opened, revealing a darkened beach.

Eglantine half-crawled, half-walked through the door, just as Miss Hegotty sent the signal and her protection flower turned into the image of a grimoire and then across the Isles, they each began to recite the counter-curse.

> *From sky above*
> *To ground below*
> *Knit our words to the bone*
> *Together as one, we stand to put things right*
> *To restore what was taken*
> *We cast our mighty Witchlight*
> *To return the magic that has been stolen*
> *To reawaken the beasts from stone*
> *With our words and our deeds*
> *So, shall it be*
> *Shine our light bright*
> *We cast our mighty Witchlight*

High up, lights began to shine, in all colours, an aurora of Witchlight that burst across the Magic Isles.

She stared at it in wonder. The light was so dazzling, she had to shade her eyes.

Hope burned brightly inside her.

Had it worked? Had they made it in time? Was the curse broken?

She sat down on the beach, her heart pounding inside her chest.

Only to see her other leg turn to stone.

Tears sprang to her eyes.

They were too late!

Her hand was growing stiff now. It too would soon turn. Her chin wobbled.

This couldn't be how it ended, could it?

Lying here on this deserted beach all alone.

All magical creatures and homes turned to lifeless stone.

It would be like ripping colour away from the world.

If she was going to turn, she didn't want it to happen here.

She needed to be with Hus.

The portal doorway back to Hus flickered, almost winking out completely. She crawled on her stomach through the sand to get to it in time before it went out, using the last of her reserves. Inside her bag, she could hear the sound of her uncle's disembodied laughter, he was growing stronger... It sent chills down her spine. If she tried to use it now, he would break free, she was sure of it.

Using the last of her strength, she dragged herself into the doorway just before it flickered out.

She was home.

But it was too late. She felt the floor beneath her and no answering pulse of life from Hus.

Tears turned to stone down her cheeks.

Arthur was the first of the others to arrive through his portal, but like Eglantine, he stumbled, as each one of his limbs turned.

Eglantine tried to call his name, but she couldn't. They stared at each other, as they both turned fully to stone.

It was Eoin who found them like that.

What he saw brought him to his knees.

"B-but the spell worked – it must have, I saw the lights!" he gasped, as he touched Eglantine's stony face with a shaky hand. He turned to Arthur and his eyes filled with tears. Then he looked around him, and realized. Hus was gone too. It was a cold, lifeless place. The heart was gone, and he felt it go from him as well.

He pressed a knuckle to his mouth and began to shake.

The other portals didn't appear. They couldn't, he realized. Not without Hus.

As he cried, he saw the bag at Eglantine's side where the now silent genie lamp had fallen out, and he picked it up in sudden fury. There was one person who could fix this. The person who had created this nightmare in the first place. He would make him undo what he had done!

Eoin rubbed it desperately, and Lichen appeared, pouring out of the lamp in a red mist, his eyes glazed, as he spoke the genie's words: "I am a genie but you may not command from me wishes three. As my master still has one more wish to fulfil. Only then can I grant another master wishes three."

"This is all your fault!" screamed Eoin, rushing towards him, but snatching at nothing more than smoke.

Eoin didn't care. He whirled around, and tried again. Happy to punch the air in his fury.

"Look at what your greed has caused. You're a murderer!"

Lichen stared at his son. For a moment, it looked as if he would be able to fight his genie enchantment, but then he just repeated: "I am a genie, but you may not command from me wishes three. As my master still has one more wish to fulfil. Only then can I grant another master wishes three."

Eoin screeched in frustration. "This is all your fault! You took my mother from me, you made me grow up without a family! And now you've taken the one I finally found! You're a MONSTER!" he sobbed. "I *wish* just for once you would see how awful you are! All the bad things you've caused."

For a second something passed over Lichen's face, as if he could really hear his only son.

Eoin continued, "I wish that you would pay for it, once and for all! I wish you were in prison just like the Whistlewitch!"

Lichen sighed. "If my wishes were yours to command it could be, but…" He explained once again that he couldn't give Eoin the wishes.

Eoin wiped his streaming eyes with his sleeve. "Then get inside the lamp at least, and out of my sight!" he spat.

"Very well," said Lichen, vanishing once more.

Eoin fell back to the ground by his cousin's still form. "Please, Eglantine, come back. I know that you can't pick your family. Look at Lichen. He's the worst. But," he sniffed, "then there's you, and you make up for it all. You and Arthur and Hus. If I could pick anyone," he said, his voice breaking, "I'd still pick you. Please, please, please come back," he begged, placing his hand in her stone one.

He closed his eyes, and his body shook with tears.

Which is why he didn't feel it at first.

Until it happened again.

It was faint. So very faint.

There was a flicker against his hand. He looked at his hand and saw one of Eglantine's fingers, moving against his.

He sat up, then gasped. Her hand reached back for his.

He looked up. Her face was still stony, but the tear that had stilled before was rolling down her cheek.

"Oh, Eglantine, you're alive? Say you're alive!"

Her finger moved again and Eoin shouted in triumph.

"I'd choose you too, Eoin Murphy," she whispered.

"Hear, hear," said Arthur, stirring too.

There was an answering thrum from the floor.

And the sound of heavy thumping, like a dog wagging its tail, and getting ready to launch itself at its owner, as The Boots raced happily to Arthur's side.

There was a shiver and a shake and Hus roared to life.

Soon all the other portal doors appeared, and everyone rushed inside. They were all cheering and speaking at once.

"Oh, it's so good to see you looking so well, Hus especially," said Nandi.

Sorcerer Nelson doffed his tricorn.

"For a moment there I was really worried," said Myrtle. "I thought perhaps the Witchlight hadn't worked as Hus and the others turned to stone."

"I think we got there just in time. The curse hadn't had the chance to fully set when the Witchlight spread, so it was able to undo it."

"Oh that makes sense," said Myrtle. "Thank goodness it didn't get that chance."

"Well, though it was a bit *dramatic*, personally I never doubted us for a second," said Nandi with a wink.

The others laughed.

Eglantine, Eoin and Arthur looked at each other. "Oh, us too," joked Eglantine.

Eoin and Arthur chuckled.

Victoria looked at her, noting their teary faces. "What's happened?" she whispered.

"We'll tell you later," said Eglantine, as Eoin came to give them both a hug.

"Deal," said Victoria.

"I'd like to know that myself," said a voice. Eglantine turned on the spot to find her father looking at her very expectantly. "Imagine my surprise when I was sent a letter today by none other than Miss Hegotty, telling me about a curse that my own daughter had written to me about some time ago – a curse that it turns out was, in fact, affecting her, Arthur and Hus, but she decided not to mention that part?"

"I, um, I can explain," said Eglantine.

"Yes," said her father. "You can. After you've been grounded for the rest of your life!"

Eglantine looked at her father. "I didn't want you to worry."

"That's my job, silly."

She nodded. "I'm sorry." Then her lips twitched. "The thing is, as far as punishments go, I mean, being with Hus and Arthur is sort of the only place I want to be…"

He rolled his eyes, then chuckled. "You have a point. I will think of something."

"I'm sure you will," she agreed, as she ran into his arms and he hugged her tight.

Not long afterwards, Miss Hegotty arrived with more good news. Lord Ragwort and Sir Conroy were in prison.

There were cheers all around.

"But how were they able to arrest Conroy too?" asked Victoria.

"Your mother!"

"What?" cried Victoria.

"After you left, she finally saw how devious he really is – she told the royal guard to search his study and they found all sorts of letters between him and Ragwort, and even Lichen. It showed they had all been planning this – from the curse, to the fires and the king's attempted murder – for months. It seems Conroy thought that he had such a hold over your mother that if she was made regent, it would be like he was the one in charge. He'd told them all that she was his puppet and did everything he asked."

A panoply of emotions flickered on Victoria's face – from anger to sorrow and pity. "That must have been very hard for her."

Miss Hegotty nodded. "It was. I told her you would be up late tonight, with us. She wasn't thrilled, of course, but the king insisted, and, well, it appears you are allowed to stay here for the night."

Victoria smiled at Miss Hegotty. "Thank you."

Miss Hegotty winked at her.

Then she took Eglantine and Eoin to one side. "There is more than enough evidence against Lichen as well. So let me know what you want to do?"

Eglantine and Eoin looked at each other. "I have one more wish left, and its safe to use now that the curse is broken and the magic he stole is back where it belongs. I could just make him go to the Old Bailey and turn himself in," said Eglantine.

"That's too good for him. I want him to face what he's done, not be under some enchantment where he can't feel anything. He should be aware of what is happening," said Eoin.

"You're right." She looked at Eoin for a moment, thinking hard. "I will free him from his lamp using the wish. After breakfast, we'll take him to the Old Bailey. Though I do wish I had just one more wish to ensure that his cell is right next to that of the Whistlewitch."

Eoin and Miss Hegotty laughed.

Then Miss Hegotty went to have a word with Myrtle about updating her story to include all that had happened.

"I have this sense", she said with a grin, "that it might just make the front page."

"I have a sense that you're right," said Myrtle, pushing up her glasses with a smile of her own.

The party that followed went on well into the dawn.

Eglantine was delighted to see Tidbit restored to health and the little gnome smiled at her and said, "I made these especially for you." They were the posh biscuits she usually reserved for special guests.

Eglantine's eyes teared up. "Thank you, Jayne."

Tidbit frowned at her. "It's still Tidbit to you, miss," she chided.

Arthur came over and bumped her hip with his tail. "That's you told."

They looked at each other and laughed.

Eglantine looked around her and felt a rush of joy.

"We did it," she cried to her friends.

They all raised their glasses and cheered.

27

THE HUSWYVERN SCHOOL OF MODERN MAGIC

While everyone was having breakfast, Eglantine went to her room to confront her uncle one last time, alone.

She rubbed the lamp and he poured out in a haze of red mist. "I am the genie from whom you may command wishes three. I cannot turn back time, bring someone back from the dead or kill. Or grant you more wishes than your wishes three. So, think long over what is deep in your heart's desire. What shall your final wish be?"

Eglantine narrowed her eyes. "Today you're going to face what you have done. You killed an innocent person. You tried to steal my home, tried to make me feel bad about who I am because of the way I was born. You tried to kill me and Arthur and Hus. You let your son feel as if he was all alone in the world. But despite all you've done, we are still here. Eoin and I found each other. I no longer feel as if there is something wrong with me. You could have had a loving family, a home, but you chose to be this way. I should hate you; I did, once. But now I just feel sorry for you."

He stared at her blankly, and she wondered if it would have made any difference if he were under the genie enchantment or not.

She had one wish left.

She thought of Eoin. His father would never apologize for what he'd done or how he'd treated him, but he could give Eoin something else. So, at the very least, Eglantine made him do that.

"I do not wish for you to be free so that you may leave, I wish for you to be free of the genie lamp so that you will get what you deserve and take responsibility for what you should have done for Eoin."

Lichen's wrists were unbound, and the red mist dissolved. The blank look vanished from his eyes. "You?" he cried. His face contorted in anger. He screamed insults, promising that he would get his revenge, but Eglantine cast magical vines that held him tight and tuned out his words. They were meaningless now.

"Where are you taking me?" he cried as she dragged him down the stairs.

"To prison."

His eyes widened in horror when he saw the rest of the society waiting for them at the bottom of the stairs. Together they marched him to the Old Bailey, where he was formally charged, alongside Lord Ragwort, Sir Conroy and countless members of the Department who had been found to be involved in their misdeeds.

When they left the prison, they passed by a news stand, where Myrtle's story was indeed on the front page of *The Weekly Spellcast*.

A week later, the new prime minster arrived at headquarters for her first meeting with Miss Hegotty and the society.

She was a tall woman with short black hair and sharply intelligent eyes behind a pair of gold spectacles. She wore a magical hat that showcased a river boat sailing along past the Houses of Parliament.

"Congratulations, Prime Minister," said Miss Hegotty, her eyes shining as she considered the woman that had helped them expose the corruption within the Department. "Our first ever female appointment."

"Thank you," said Mrs Kusum. "I believe it was the fact that certain members of the Department had made it their secret mission to bind the magic of so many girls that helped win me the vote. Not to mention the fact that my supporters and I had been quietly trying to build a case against Ragwort and his crooked accomplices."

"I am glad," said Miss Hegotty.

Arthur came in with a fresh pot of tea, followed by The Boots. Myrtle took a sip of tea, then fished out her truth catcher.

Mrs Kusum looked on in wonder. "'Tis a most remarkable

house," she said. "In fact," she continued, "you are all remarkable, and we owe you a great debt." She looked from Miss Hegotty to everyone gathered around the table. "It is my honour to offer your society a reward, for exposing the corruption in our government. We wish you to know that what Lord Ragwort and his associates did – how they used the Department for their own ends – is not a reflection of our government, and we will strive at all costs to make it something the nation can trust once again."

There was pause, and Myrtle exclaimed, "She is telling the truth!", holding the truth catcher up for them all to see where Mrs Kusum's words had caused the catcher to glow – a sign that it had recorded the truth.

Mrs Kusum's eyes widened.

"Sorry," said Myrtle, blushing.

Mrs Kusum waved a hand. "I can understand the surprise. Politicians generally are not known for their truth telling, but I assure you, I am not like most politicians."

Eglantine noticed that the woman looked tired. No doubt she had been busy dealing with the fallout of what Lichen, Lord Ragwort and Conroy had done, and with the public outcry that had followed after the newspaper article revealed the truth.

It was the last thought that made Eglantine look at Arthur and say, "What about magical creatures, Mrs Kusum?"

"Yes," agreed Arthur. "Is there a way for us all to work together?"

"I believe so," said Mrs Kusum. "We are in talks with magical creatures to build a more inclusive, fair government for all. We've appointed some into ministry positions, so that from now on everyone in the Isles is represented."

This wasn't that surprising. After the creatures found out what had happened to them, how they had almost been wiped out, the government were afraid that they would retaliate. Many of the laws that had been put into place that restricted their rights were abolished. The government was now working closely with the Union of Magical Creatures to ensure that there were equal rights for all.

Victoria, on the other hand, had been waiting for over a week on the decision of what parliament would say after they discovered that she was a witch.

"Your Highness," continued Mrs Kusum. "After much deliberation, parliament have decided that *one* crisis is enough and we have had a long look at the rule that royals shouldn't have magic, and decided that just because there was one king, in the past, who abused his powers, doesn't mean that all will…"

"That's what I always said!" exclaimed Eoin.

Mrs Kusum nodded. "Quite right."

"You mean…I will be allowed to stay on? I don't have to give up the crown?" said Victoria, her mouth falling open in shock and happiness.

Mrs Kusum gave her a wry smile. "Well, it wasn't that hard to sell…" she admitted. "Considering the fact that when the Union of Magical Creatures found out it was the *future queen* who helped to break the curse against them, they vowed to protect you to the death. The government, rather wisely, decided that having a royal with magic is probably better than starting a war with the country's dragons, wyverns and gargoyles…"

"Wise indeed," said Arthur, his lips twitching.

Mrs Kusum grinned at him. Then she turned to Miss Hegotty.

"So, what shall it be? We cannot let this debt go unrewarded. Would you all like a financial gift? The king, who thanks you for saving his life, is, as you can imagine, feeling very generous, and has suggested a title and property."

"No," said Miss Hegotty.

"Let's not get hasty now," joked Eoin.

They all laughed.

Mrs Kusum looked at Eoin, and said, "You are Eoin Murphy, son of Lord Lichen Bury?"

"How did you know?"

"Shortly after your father was sentenced at the Old Bailey, he signed over his home and assets to his son, Eoin Murphy, acknowledging that you are his heir."

Eoin looked floored. "But…why?'" He glanced at Eglantine, who was very pointedly not looking at him, her cheeks flushed.

He frowned. "I…I didn't even want that, I just wanted him to admit to what he'd done."

"Well, the evidence was enough, even if he wouldn't admit to it. So perhaps this is his way of acknowledging his guilt. I can't tell you what to do with your new wealth, but I would say, you could put it to better use, do some good with it. Just food for thought."

"I agree," said Eglantine.

Eoin looked at her again. Then slowly he began to chuckle. "Oh, I *see*."

She winked back at him and they smiled.

Sneaky, he mouthed.

Eglantine shrugged. She didn't feel even a little bit bad. It was only what Eoin deserved.

Mrs Kusum looked at Miss Hegotty. "Financial rewards could help a great many worthy causes..."

Miss Hegotty shook her head. "I can't speak for everyone, but what I'd most like is for my course to no longer be banned, and for schools across the Isles to begin teaching some of my methods. We could use them to unbind children's magic and teach others how to discover their Witchspark," said Miss Hegotty, who in her heart of hearts, really was a teacher first and foremost.

Mrs Kusum swallowed. It looked like she had hoped that Miss Hegotty would ask for something easier.

But after a while, she nodded. "We can remove the ban from your course and begin with some of what you suggested – the method to unbind children's magic is something I can put forward. Witchspark – well, that may take some time. I am not sure we will be able to roll that out just yet. Change is possible but perhaps we can begin with one school," she said. "A school of your own. Teaching your...modern approach to witchcraft?"

Mss Hegotty's eyes widened.

"My own school?" She seemed to ponder the idea, and then she smiled.

Eglantine felt Hus's response, the way it shivered with excitement. "You can have it here," she suggested.

"Here? Really?"

"Yes," she said. "It's what Hus would like. But only if I get to enrol," she said. "I quite like the idea of Miss Hegotty's School for Revolutionary Witches…"

"Me too," cried Myrtle, Nandi, Victoria and Eoin.

"Um…" said Mrs Kusum, blanching somewhat. "I – well. Maybe a title just a tad less extreme, erm…"

"Perhaps," agreed Miss Hegotty. "I also feel the title honour should go to dear Huswyvern, not me."

There was a delighted thrumming from the floor, and the coat rack seemed to shimmy.

Suddenly, there was the sound of tinkling bricks, then a saw, followed by the sound of drilling.

"What on earth?" cried Mrs Kusum.

Eglantine could feel Hus's excitement.

"It's Hus, it wants to show us something!" she cried, as their chairs tipped them out, and the floors slid beneath their feet, pushing them all into a run as they were ushered outside, where a sign read:

The Huswyvern School of Modern Magic.

Everyone cheered.

Eglantine looked at her friends, and touched the wall of her beloved home.

It was *perfect*.

Acknowledgements

So many people help bring a book into the world, and I am so grateful to each and every one who helped bring *Witchlight* to life.

My wonderful agent, Helen Boyle, thank you for being the absolute best, for making the story better, being an absolute dream to work with and just the best human, thank you!

My editors, Rebecca Hill and Amelia Mehra. Rebecca, it is such an honour to work with you, and I have learned so much. I'm incredibly grateful and in awe of your lovely brain.

Amelia, working with you this past year has been an absolute delight! This has been one of my favourite edits ever, thanks to you. Thank you for all your kindness, support and your eagle-eyed fixes – you are a marvel.

To the incredibly talented Eleonora Asparuhova for your utterly gorgeous artwork. You are amazing, and I am so lucky to work with you.

To Debbie Sims and Charlotte James for the top-notch editorial skills.

Will Steele for the beautiful cover design. I love it.

Sarah Cronin for the stunning interior design.

Hannah Reardon-Steward for her marketing, Fritha Lindqvist for publicity and for all the fun – getting to know you has been so amazing. Thank you for being so lovely.

To Jessica Feichtlbauer and the rest of the Usborne team for being so amazing, thank you.

My wonderful husband, Rui, for all the pep talks whenever I got overwhelmed and began to doubt myself, and for always believing in me.

There is nothing more surreal than when some of your favourite authors read and enjoy your books, and when news started to arrive that some of these incredible authors enjoyed *Witchspark*, and were kind enough to say lovely things about it, I almost thought my publishers were making it up, but they have assured me it was true. So thank you, from the bottom of my heart, to the incredible Annaliese Avery, Laura Ellen Anderson, Katya Balen, Jennifer Bell, Jack Meggitt-Phillips, Elle McNicoll, Vashti Hardy, Nicola Baker, Bex Hogan, Maisie Chan, Katherine Woodfine and Harry Woodgate.

Huge thank you to Vashti Hardy, Jennifer Bell and Bex Hogan for their wonderful words about *Witchlight*, I am so thrilled you enjoyed being back with Eglantine, Hus and the gang!

To all the bookshops who have supported me and my books, thank you so much. To Dial Lane Books – you guys are the stuff dreams are made of. Thank you for being so wonderful and supportive. Stillwater Books in Felixstowe, my local treasure, thank you for everything you do. Woodbridge Books, you guys are just the best.

Last but not least to you, the reader, thank you so much! It's thanks to you that I get to keep writing. Your support means the world. To all the amazing people who have left kind reviews and posted lovely things online, the wonderful parents who read with their kids, the kids who dress up as my characters for World Book Day or write me letters or create artwork to send to me, you have made this author so happy – thank you so much! If you enjoyed this story, please consider leaving a review. They really help spread the word and make such a difference to a book's success. I'd so appreciate it.

DOMINIQUE VALENTE is the author of the best-selling *Starfell* series, and her unique voice and brand of quirky magic has found fans amongst readers and booksellers across the globe. She lives in Suffolk, in a (sadly non-magical) house with her husband and dog. Find out more at dominiquevalente.com or @dominiquevalente on Instagram.

Discover where Eglantine and Victoria's story began in *WITCHSPARK*.